—The—
Chimney Sweep's Ransom

Trailblazer Books

TITLE	HISTORIC CHARACTERS
Kidnapped by River Rats	William & Catherine Booth
The Queen's Smuggler	William Tyndale
Spy for the Night Riders	Doctor Martin Luther
The Hidden Jewel	Amy Carmichael
Escape from the Slave Traders	David Livingstone
The Chimney Sweep's Ransom	John Wesley

–The–
Chimney Sweep's Ransom

DAVE & NETA JACKSON

Illustrated by
Julian Jackson

BETHANY HOUSE PUBLISHERS
MINNEAPOLIS, MINNESOTA 55438

Published by Bethany House Publishers
A Ministry of Bethany Fellowship, Inc.
6820 Auto Club Road, Minneapolis, Minnesota 55438

Printed in the United States of America

Library of Congress Cataloging-in-Publication Data

Jackson, Dave.
    The chimney sweep's ransom / Dave & Neta Jackson ; [inside illustrations by Julian Jackson].
        p. cm. — (Trailblazer Books)
    Summary: While searching for his younger brother who has been "sold" to be trained as a chimney sweep in eighteenth-century London, thirteen-year-old Ned meets the itinerant preacher John Wesley whose message changes the lives of his entire family.
    [1. Children—Employment—Fiction. 2. Coal mines and mining—Fiction. 3. Chimney sweeps—Fiction. 4. Wesley, John 1703–1791—Fiction 5. Christian life—Fiction. 6. England—Fiction.]
I. Jackson, Neta. II. Jackson, Julian, ill. III. Title. IV. Series.
PZ7.J132418Ch   1992
[Fic]—dc20   92–546
ISBN 1–55661–268–0   CIP
                                        AC

John Wesley, founder of the Methodist movement, first visited Newcastle-upon-Tyne in 1742, where he found conditions among the mining families some of the worst in all England. Many true events and facts about John Wesley, his travels, and the Methodist Societies have been woven throughout this story. The Carter family, though fictional, represents the plight faced by many poor families in this region—children as young as five years old went to work in the mines, and were often "sold" for five pounds as chimney sweeps.

DAVE AND NETA JACKSON are a husband/wife writing team who have authored or coauthored many books on marriage and family, the church, and relationships, including *On Fire for Christ: Stories from Martyrs Mirror*, the Pet Parables series, and the Caring Parent series.

They have two children: Julian, an art major and illustrator for the Trailblazer series, and Rachel, a high school student. They make their home in Evanston, Illinois, where they are active members of Reba Place Church.

CONTENTS

Chapter 1

Mule Driver

NED CARTER SLAPPED THE REINS against the rumps of the mules he was driving and hunched his shoulders against the chilly drizzle. "Yup! Yup!" he yelled. "You mules gonna stand in the mud all day? Move! Move!"

The coal wagon groaned as it lurched forward again. September had arrived in northern England, and it had been drizzling for a week. The dirt road leading from the coal mines on the outskirts of Newcastle down to the docks on the Tyne River had become a sea of mud.

People crowded the road leading into Newcastle, making it even more difficult to drive the mules. Ned swore under his breath. Papa would be coming along any minute with another wagon load of coal and if

Ned wasn't even past the town gate, he'd be angry.

A familiar figure darted across the road ahead of the coal wagon, carrying a large basket on one hip. Effie! Stupid girl. Why was his sister delivering Mama's laundry in the rain? It would be damp and muddy by the time she arrived at the customer in town.

Just then Ned saw a tall boy catch up to his sister and take the basket of laundry. Effie looked up into the boy's face coyly as the two of them made their way into the market. Immediately Ned felt hot anger. That stuck-up Morgan what's-his-name . . . still chasing Effie. She encouraged him, too. Just because his father was a merchant in Newcastle didn't impress Ned. Next thing they knew, she'd do something foolish like run off with that rich kid and get married. She was only sixteen—three years older than Ned—but some girls married even younger than that.

Without thinking, Ned yelled "Whoa!" to the mules, pulled the wagon brake, and jumped to the ground. *Where did they go?* The boy sprinted across the muddy ruts toward the town gate, shoving his way past farmers and tradesmen all heading for Newcastle's large market square. The crowd was even thicker inside the gate and Ned was afraid he'd lost the pair . . . no, there they were, taking shelter in a doorway.

He was upon them before they saw him coming. He grabbed Effie's arm and jerked her out of the doorway.

"You tramp!" he snarled at his sister. Ned was big and strong for thirteen and glared at her straight in the face. "Mama works all day slaving over that laundry and you stand here flirting with this stupid goat-face while the clothes get wet."

"Hey, now . . ." protested the boy named Morgan.

"Leave me alone, Ned Carter!" yelled Effie, jerking her arm away. But this time he grabbed her hair and jerked so hard she nearly fell down.

"I'm going to tell Papa what you're doing!" Ned shouted in her ear. "What are we gonna do if we lose customers who don't like wet laundry? You want little Pip to work in the mines? Is that what you want? You selfish pig!"

Effie's fingernails scratching his face stopped his yelling. He let go of her hair, and she gave him a shove. Caught off guard, Ned tumbled to the ground. When he looked up, Effie, Morgan, and the basket of laundry were disappearing around a corner.

Ned scrambled to his feet, then realized he'd lost his cap. He looked this way and that, and finally saw it flattened in the street by a passing wagon wheel.

He had just snatched up the cap when he felt a painful cuff on his ear that sent him sprawling to the ground again; then he was hauled up by his shirt collar.

"What's this?" his father roared. "What do you mean leavin' the coal wagon sitting in the road with no driver? I'll stick you back down in the mine shaft quicker'n you can say doomsday if you ever leave that wagon again, you scalawag!"

"But, Papa—!" Ned started to protest. Then he saw the humorous glances being cast in his direction. Humiliated, he shut his mouth and marched back through the town gate to the coal wagon; his father—grim-faced and thick-shouldered—followed right on his heels.

Ned scrambled onto the wagon, kicked the brake free, and gee-hawed the mules into action before Dob Carter could say more. Ned's anger at Effie had been rattled right out of him . . . but in its place a gnawing fear began to take shape, not of the tongue-lashing he knew he would get when he got home that night, but fear for his little brother, Pip.

Pip had turned five that spring. So far nothing

had been said about taking the youngest Carter boy away from his mother and putting him to work. But Ned had been just five years old when his father had taken him to the coal mines to work as a "mole." He would never forget the terror of crawling into a narrow mine shaft for the first time, a rope tied to his ankles so he could be pulled out, the darkness so thick and black he could hardly breathe.

For seven years Ned had worked the mines, getting up before sunrise with his father and trudging across the bridge that joined Gateshead, on the south side of the river, and Newcastle, on the north, into one large town. By the time they passed Newcastle's town gate, they had joined the great flood of men and boys who pulled coal—the life-blood of England—from the earth.

Every day he worked alongside Dob Carter, filling buckets as his father hacked coal veins with a pick axe, hauling stones, smoothing roads that wound down into the yawning open pit, loading wagons. More than once Ned and his father had barely escaped injury—or death—when a shaft caved in or flooded, or a mule slipped and a heavy wagon crashed down the side of the pit, crushing everyone in its path. Ned and his father had an unspoken agreement never to mention these narrow escapes to Ned's mother.

A year ago Dob Carter had been promoted to wagon master, and Ned had learned to drive mules. He liked driving the heavy wagon loads of coal down to the docks, where it was loaded onto keel-boats and ferried to the big ships anchored in mid-river.

Yes, Ned had survived—but Pip was different. His little brother had never been very strong, and looked a year younger than other children his age. He was also a dreamer, content to sing little songs and make up stories as he sat in a corner by himself. There was no way Pip would survive in the mines.

The wagon gave a lurch, interrupting Ned's thoughts. The mules had begun the descent down the sloping river bank toward the long row of docks jutting out like fingers into the Tyne. Ned tightened his grip on the reins. "Steady, now, Bessie. Easy goes it, Ben," he crooned as the mules searched for firm footing in the mud.

Half-way down the slope, Bessie's hooves slipped and she went down on her knees. Ben, the other mule, gave a frightened whinny and reared back, trying to pull up his teammate. The wagon pitched to one side and Ned grabbed for the brake, trying to keep the wagon from tipping over. After an anxious moment, Bessie scrambled up again, the wagon settled back into the muddy rut, and they continued the slippery descent to the docks.

Ned let out a relieved whistle. *Sure wish the rain would stop making a mud slide out of this river bank,* he thought. *Next time we might not be so lucky.*

Chapter 2

The Slippery Slope

WHEN NED WOKE the next morning, he could tell by the drips coming through the ceiling that the fine misty rain had not stopped. It was still dark outside, but he could see his mother bent over the cooking fire, stirring a big pot. Easing himself off the straw mattress he shared with Pip, Ned used the chamber pot behind the curtain in the corner of the two-room cottage, buttoned his braces, and slid onto the bench alongside the table.

Louisa Carter set a big steaming bowl of oatmeal in the center of the table and handed Ned a spoon. "Eat hearty, lad," she said, touching him briefly on the shoulder. "Only one more day till the day of rest."

Ned looked at the big bowl. Oatmeal again. Oatmeal every single breakfast for as long as he could remember. He glanced around the table . . . no milk, either. At least some mornings they had milk.

He remembered the eggs someone had given them last Christmas. His mouth watered thinking of the golden yolk hidden inside that hot boiled egg. *I bet that stuck-up Morgan what's-his-name has eggs for breakfast every day,* Ned thought with a scowl.

Dob Carter sat down on the bench on the other side of the table, plunged his spoon into the common bowl in the center, and lifted a steaming spoonful to his mouth. "Eat," he grunted at Ned. "It ain't Sunday yet. We've got a day's wage to earn."

Effie appeared at the table, followed by Flora, age ten, tousled and yawning. Soon seven-year-old Dolly, lugging fat baby Gilda in her arms, also crawled onto the bench.

"Pip!" Dob Carter barked. "Will you forever be last? The time for breakfast is *now*." Within a few moments Pip, undaunted by his father's gruffness, knelt on the bench beside the big man and thrust his spoon into the bowl.

The warmth of the oatmeal filled Ned's stomach, easing the chill in the damp cottage. He watched as his mother wearily picked up little Gilda, almost two years old now, and sat on a chair by the fire, nursing her. His mother looked pale and haggard in the firelight.

"Papa, Mama doesn't look so good," Ned said across the table. "Tell the girls to do what needs to be done today, and let Mama rest—"

"Speak for yourself," Effie muttered under her breath.

Dob Carter looked over at his wife. "Lou?"

Louisa Carter was silent for a few moments. Then she sighed, "I'll be all right. Just having trouble getting over that cold I had last week."

Ned's father got up from the table and put on his jacket and cap. He laid a heavy hand on Pip's small shoulder, not unkindly. "You help your ma and the girls, you hear? You must learn how to work hard." Pip, his mouth full of oatmeal, beamed at his father and nodded.

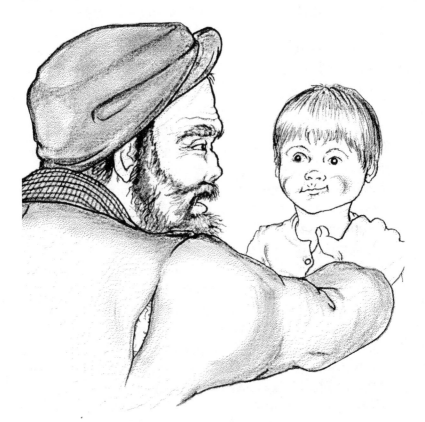

Ned picked up the pail with the bread and cold cooked potatoes his mother had packed for their noon dinner. It was the same every day. As he started for the door, Effie deliberately bumped into him.

"Stick to your own business and quit trying to run my life," she hissed in his ear. "I'm the oldest around here, remember?" Then she flounced away and began clearing the breakfast table.

Ned glared at his sister, then hurried out the door after his father. The gray sky was just starting to get light. As father and son walked the narrow streets of Gateshead toward the bridge over the Tyne, Ned realized it wasn't really raining, but a heavy mist hung in the air, as if the earth was sweating from every pore.

They joined other men and boys who were coming out of a long wooden building: the miner's barracks. The Carter family had lived in one of these barracks—one great long room with every few feet sectioned off for each family. There was absolutely no privacy; men, women, and children cooking, eating, sleeping, having babies, crying, laughing, playing, fighting—all together in the filthy soot.

Ned remembered his mother's joy when Dob Carter scrimped together enough money to rent their two-room cottage after Pip was born. Of her eight babies, only five had survived. When she recovered from Pip's birth, Louisa Carter had to take in washing from the merchants' wives in Newcastle or they wouldn't be able to pay the rent. The tiny cottage was often a maze of laundry hanging up to dry by the fire on damp days—which was most of the time. But the family was patient; it seemed like a palace after having lived in the barracks.

Then Mrs. Carter became pregnant again. It was a difficult pregnancy, and Ned thought his mother never really recovered after Gilda was born. She always seemed to be tired or have a cold. But Mama and the girls continued taking in laundry; there was no choice. Ned often saw his father looking at his wife with a worried look, but Dob Carter said little. No one—least of all Louisa Carter—wanted to move back into the barracks.

As the long line of miners trudged over the bridge, a crowd seemed to be gathering around the town gate of Newcastle. Ned craned his neck to see what was happening.

"There's a man standing on a box, talking to everybody," Ned said. "What's happening, Papa?" Father and son stopped for a moment, as did many of the others, curious at this diversion in the dull morning routine.

The crowd jostled and coughed and Ned had to strain to hear what the man was saying. Finally he began to catch some of the words.

". . . you may be an honest man, a good man, who is kind to his family and his neighbors," the man on the box was saying. "You may go to church every week, and obey all the commandments. You have a form of godliness. In this you may be an *almost* Christian. But what does God require to be *altogether* a Christian? You must love God with all your heart, and believe—"

"Eh! Just some preacher," snorted Dob Carter, spitting in disgust. "Religion is a luxury for the rich." He took Ned by the arm and pulled him away from the crowd.

Ned shrugged and fell into step with his father. He didn't care one way or the other and soon forgot the strange man on the box as his thoughts drifted back to his mother's worn face by the firelight. . . . What if Mama got sick? Or what if Effie really did run off with that snobby merchant's son? The younger girls would never be able to keep up with the heavy loads of washing from paying customers. How long could Papa afford to let Pip stay at home?

The scowl on Ned's face deepened. Whatever happened, he would fight to keep his little brother out of the mine.

Ned had little time to think about his worries once they arrived at the mine. The mules were cranky and took every ounce of the thirteen-year-old's concentration to keep them moving with their load of coal down to the docks. The morning mist, instead of breaking up, had settled into a fog so thick Ned could hardly see the road in front of Bessie's and Ben's noses.

Ned was worried as he headed down the muddy road to the docks. An enormous rut had been developing in the center of the road, worn deep by wagons both going down and coming up. With a lot of gee-hawing and hauling on the reins, however, the boy was able to keep his mules off to the side of the rut, crowding the bank that rose toward the town. A few minutes later he finally pulled up beside the river docks.

"Back it up!" yelled one of the dock hands. Grimly, Ned carefully backed the mules and wagon onto the dock. It was hard to judge how far to back in the fog. One misstep and Ned was afraid wagon and mules— along with himself—would go tumbling into the river. But finally the tailgate hung over the end of the dock just above the keel-boat. Working quickly, the dock hands shoveled the entire load onto the boat, then waved him on. Relieved, Ned drove away from the dock and started back up the river bank road.

He passed his father who was waiting to back his own wagon load of coal onto the docks. Dob Carter gave Ned a nod as he passed. Ned smiled inwardly; his father seemed to have forgotten his anger about Ned leaving the coal wagon yesterday. Well, he wouldn't abandon the wagon again . . . but that Morgan fellow better leave Effie alone if he knew what was good for him.

Going up the hill, Ned had to drive on the side of the road that dropped off toward the river. Not wanting to get too close to the edge, he drove the wagon as close as he dared to the center rut. Halfway up the hill, however, the wagon began slipping sideways into the rut.

"Gee-haw, you mules!" Ned yelled, slapping the reins. "Pull! Pull!" Bessie and Ben leaned into their harnesses, but the wagon kept slipping sideways until the rear right wheel settled into the deep rut. The mules scrambled and strained, but the wagon slowed, then creaked to a stop.

Ned let loose with a string of swear words. Stuck!

He jumped off the empty wagon and stared at the rear wheel, nearly hub-deep in mud. He glanced down toward the docks, but they were hidden in the fog. By now his father's wagon would be nearly emptied by the dock hands, and Dob Carter would be coming up the road any minute. Frantically, the boy fell to his knees and began scooping mud away from the wheel.

The sticky muck seemed to cling fiercely to the

wooden spokes, but soon Ned had most of it cleared away. Another driver, coming down the hill, saw Ned's predicament and offered to help. The man leaned his shoulder against the rear of the wagon while Ned climbed back up in the wagon seat.

"Haw!" he yelled at the mules. "Gee-haw!"

Bessie and Ben strained and pulled, but for a moment nothing happened. Then suddenly the wheel jerked free with such a jolt that Ned flew backward off the seat. He struck his head—hard—against the side of the wagon as he fell to the ground. A sharp pain shot up his arm. Then . . . everything went black.

Chapter 3

No Work, No Wages

NED! NED! CAN YOU HEAR me, lad?"

It was his father's voice, sounding urgent and far away.

Ned opened his eyes. Two concerned faces hung over him. He was lying in the mud beside the wagon wheel. Then he remembered: he'd fallen off the wagon.

Embarrassed, the boy struggled to sit up, but a sharp pain in his right arm made him wince and fall back.

"He'll come around, Dob," said the man who had stopped his team to help push Ned's wagon out of the mud. "That there wheel rolled over his arm—better have it checked out. But I think the rest of him is going to be all right."

Ned felt his father's big hands lift his shoulders from the mud. "Here, Jenkins—help me get him in the wagon." Ned was carefully lifted from the mud and placed in the back of the wagon. Small, sharp pieces of coal littering the bed of the wagon stuck to the wet mud on his back. Painfully, Ned pushed himself up until he was leaning against the side of the wagon.

Dob Carter climbed into the driver's seat and slapped the reins on the mules' backs. The coal wagon rattled to life. Topping the hill, it rumbled past the town walls of Newcastle, then turned over the bridge to Gateshead. Ned realized his father was taking him home.

Ned twisted his head from side to side. Ouch! He had a big lump on the side of his head where he'd hit the wagon. He flexed first one leg, then the other, then his left arm; all right there. But his right arm lay throbbing in his lap.

He watched his father's broad back as Dob Carter drove on in silence. Besides the pain, Ned was scared. How could he drive the coal wagon now? What was wrong with his arm? Was his father angry at him for being careless? With a sinking heart Ned realized what a mess he'd created. Not only was he no good for work the rest of the day, but his father had had to leave his own wagon in order to bring him home.

The coal wagon with its dejected passenger pulled up in front of the Carter cottage. Pip and the younger girls ran out, surprised to see their father in the middle of the day. Louisa Carter and Effie followed.

"Ned, here, got himself hurt," Dob Carter said grimly, helping Ned slide off the wagon into his mother's anxious arms. Climbing back into the driver's seat, Dob leaned toward his wife. "Do what you can for him, Lou—but don't pay out money for the doctor. It ain't a matter of life and death."

As the coal wagon headed back toward the river, Louisa Carter helped Ned inside the cottage. It was steamy with damp clothes hanging to dry. He sat on the straw pallet while his mother's fingers probed his arm gently. She moved it at the shoulder, then gingerly at the elbow.

"Your hand is swelling," she said, touching the puffy skin. "I think the wrist is broken." She sent Pip running to the well for a bucket of cool water and ordered Ned to soak his hand while she prepared a poultice.

While their mother was busy tearing strips of cloth for a bandage, Effie loomed over him, hands on her hips. "Ain't this dandy," she said. "Now the big man of the family can't work."

"Scat, cat!" he hissed at her. He felt bad enough without Effie's scorn.

Ned watched his mother closely as she wrapped his hand with the strips of cloth soaked in the poultice. He didn't like the pale, clammy look of her skin, and her eyes were unusually bright.

"Mama . . . ?"

"Hush!" she said sharply, resting his arm in a sling and tying it around his neck. "I've got plenty to do without answering a lot of questions. Now, you

stay there and keep that arm still while the bandage
stiffens, you hear?"

Ned lay back on the straw pallet, his mind dulled
by the throbbing pain, and the warm, damp air in
the cottage. Images floated in and out of his mind:
the mules straining in their harness. . . lying in the
mud almost beneath the wagon wheel . . . shirts and
sheets hanging ghostlike in the little cottage . . . little
Gilda patting his head . . . tubs of wash water being
filled and emptied . . . the rise and fall of familiar
voices all around him . . . .

✧ ✧ ✧ ✧

Ned woke with a start. Dob Carter was silhouetted against the cooking fire, his back toward the straw pallet.

"Wrist broken you say? The fool!" His father slapped his cap against his coal-blackened pants. "What'll it be—two, maybe three weeks till he can drive the mules? What? *Six?*"

Ned couldn't hear his mother's murmured reply. But Dob Carter paced up and down in front of the fire.

"If he can't work, he won't get wages, neither. I don't see any way around it, Lou. I gotta put Pip to work."

"No!" Louisa Carter's voice rose sharply.

Ned struggled up from the mattress as best he could with one arm. "No, Papa!" he said, alarmed. "My arm'll get better fast. I'll be back driving mules before you know it!"

Dob Carter turned and glared at him. "That's right, you will! But ain't no way it's going to happen tomorrow or next week. And this family is hanging by a thread as it is."

Louisa Carter was crying. "Not the mines, Dob! Not Pip. He—"

"Didn't say the mines, did I?" Ned's father snapped. "Got something in mind, gonna check it out. But quit the crying and begging, Lou. What's happened has happened; ain't no way around it no more." With that, Dob Carter pulled his cap back on and stomped out of the house, leaving a deadly silence in the air.

Effie put supper on the table: barley bread and potato soup, flavored with salt pork, carrots and turnips. Ned ate awkwardly from the common bowl with his left hand, causing Gilda and Dolly to giggle. Pip watched him with wide eyes over his spoon; Ned looked away.

Louisa Carter left the food untouched and disappeared into the smaller room which served as a bedroom for the Carter parents and baby Gilda. The children ate in silence. Exhausted by the effort, Ned returned to the pallet and fell into a sound sleep.

He awoke to Effie shaking his good shoulder. "Ned! Ned! Wake up! Papa hasn't come home and Mama is sick."

Ned was instantly awake. He saw Pip curled up at his feet, sleeping, the end of the blanket pulled around his thin body. The fire was down, just a few red embers still glowing in the night. Ned sat up, wincing as pain shot up to his shoulder, and followed Effie into the smaller room. A candle sputtered on a small table. Louisa Carter was lying on the bed wrapped in a blanket, her body shaking with chills, her hair damp with sweat.

"Y-your father," she said between chattering teeth. "Hasn't c-c-come home. Something may have happened. G-got to find him."

"The fever," Effie mouthed at Ned silently.

Ned leaned close to his mother and stroked her hair with his left hand. "I'll look for him, Mama. Don't you worry." He already had a good idea where to find his father.

"Not alone . . . t-t-together. You and Effie find him."

Effie woke ten-year-old Flora to come sit with their mother and showed her how to wipe the sick woman's face with a cool cloth. Ned struggled into his jacket, leaving the right sleeve flapping loosely, while Effie pulled a shawl around her head and shoulders. Then the brother and sister quietly slipped outside the house into the night.

"Look. Stars are out," said Effie. "Maybe it's a good sign."

Ned grunted. Things couldn't get much worse in his opinion. Mama sick, his arm hurt like fire, Papa threatening to put Pip to work and probably drunk to boot . . . . The boy put feet to his thoughts and plodded steadily through the dark streets. Hurrying to keep up, Effie grabbed on to the empty sleeve of Ned's jacket.

Turning down a narrow street near the river, the two young Carters were confronted with laughter and lights spilling out of a noisy tavern. A weathered sign hanging over the door read, "Pete's Publick Pub." Effie hung back a little, but Ned stepped into the smoky room and looked around.

"Hey, Carter!" he heard a voice yell. "It's your youngun'."

Heads swiveled. Ned's eyes swept the room but didn't immediately recognize the face he was looking for. Then a husky figure half rose from a table back in a corner.

"What youngun'? Don' have no youngun'. Sol' 'em

all down river. Now I'm rich . . . Hey, Pete. 'Nother gin!"

It was Dob Carter, dead drunk.

"Sure you did, Carter!" Several of the men guffawed. "But this one's coming' for ya—hey! An' your girl, too. Now, ain't she a purty thing."

Effie had followed Ned uncertainly into the tavern but now wished she hadn't. Ned grabbed her arm and pulled her over to their father.

"Papa, you've gotta come home with us. Mama's bad sick," Ned said urgently. He tried to help his father stand. "Come on."

"Bad sick, y'say?" Dob Carter stared vacantly at his two oldest children. "Nah—"

"Yes, Papa!" Effie said. "It's the fever. She needs you."

Overhearing the children, the tavern owner helped them get Dob Carter out the door and started down the street. The drunk man leaned heavily on Ned's shoulder. Painfully, Ned tried to shift his weight, but it was an awkward trio that staggered through the night toward the little cottage.

Chapter 4

The Little Giant

DOB CARTER DID NOT WAKE UP from his drunken stupor until noon on the next day—Sunday. When Ned had told his mother that Papa was safely home by the fire (sprawled on the floor, to be exact), the sick woman had fallen into a fitful sleep as well.

When he finally roused himself, Mr. Carter was distressed. "Lou? Sick? Why didn't you wake me?" The big man, still a bit unsteady, sat beside his wife all afternoon, bathing her face with a cool cloth to keep the fever down, and giving her sips of water. The other children, under Effie and Ned's supervision, kept the fire going, did chores, put food on the table, and comforted little Gilda who wanted her mother. Effie tried to shoo the younger ones outside to play in the sunshine finally breaking through the gray September clouds. But, worried about their mother, all they did was sit on the doorstep.

Twilight had settled over the river town when Dob Carter finally came out of the little bedroom and lowered himself into the chair by the fire. "The fever broke," he said wearily. He sat for a long time staring into the flames.

Ned, worn out by the midnight search for his father and the day's long vigil, lay exhausted on his pallet. Everything seemed wrong, but he was too tired and his arm hurt too much to try and figure it out.

The following morning—Monday—he awoke at the usual time before daybreak. For a moment he expected to hear his father's gruff voice telling him it was time to go to work; then he remembered. He couldn't drive the coal wagon, or do anything else at the mine for that matter, for several weeks.

Easing himself off the pallet so as to not wake Pip, Ned quietly slipped out the door into the half-light that precedes the dawn. He felt restless and guilty. He had to go somewhere . . . do something. He didn't want to be around when his father headed for the mine alone. With Mama sick, too . . . if only there was something he could do!

He found himself walking the familiar route across the bridge and past Newcastle's town gate. But instead of heading toward the mine, Ned wandered into the countryside. Wildflowers dripped with morning dew along the lane. Somewhere a rooster crowed, answered by another. Then he heard the friendly cackle of a hen.

Ned's mouth watered. Eggs! That was it. He'd snitch a few eggs and take them home to Mama for breakfast. Wouldn't that make her feel better! He'd have to make up some story about how he got them; she'd be hopping mad if she knew he stole them.

Once his mind was made up, Ned awkwardly climbed over the sod fence and made his way toward the first farmyard. He almost forgot his throbbing wrist, hugged in its sling to his chest, as he crept quietly toward some rough-hewn hay racks. That was a likely place for hens to make their nests.

He was startled when a dog barked close behind him. But, surprisingly, the shaggy mutt came toward him wagging its tail and panting happily. Ned patted the floppy ears, then reached his good hand into a shadowy hole in the hay. Success! He lifted out a warm egg and cradled it in his injured hand.

Two eggs . . . three . . . four . . . then he encountered a stubborn hen who gave him a good peck and began squawking. Maybe four was all he could carry anyway. Giving the dog another quick pat, Ned scurried back across the dew-wet field, over the sod fence, and back toward town.

Carrying the four eggs carefully in his two hands, Ned trotted home. It was fully light now. The sky was overcast again, but the clouds were high; maybe they'd get some more sunshine today. His father should be at the mine by now, but he kept a quick eye out, just in case.

As he neared the bridge, Ned saw that a crowd

had gathered again near the town gate. Was it that fool preacher again? Ned wiggled into the crowd. Sure enough . . . and what a little man he was! Couldn't be an inch taller than Ned himself. The man had to stand on a box to raise himself high enough to be seen by the crowd, and then just barely.

Ned edged closer. Weren't preachers supposed to preach in church? Not that he'd ever been in church; his father said that churches weren't for the likes of the Carters.

". . . God's gift of salvation is for rich and poor alike," the preacher was booming. He sure had a big voice for such a small man.

"Tell that to the rich folks, Rev'ren'!" shouted someone in the crowd sarcastically.

"Yeah!" shouted another voice. "They act like they got the salvation market cornered! Them and their fancy churches and expensive Sunday clothes."

"But, my good man, that is the Good News," the preacher boomed. "Each one of you—man, woman, and child—can have the gift of God's salvation by faith alone. God loves—"

"Oh, sure 'E does," sneered the first voice. "That's why my missus died leavin' me with six younguns."

"Workin' the pit mines is another blessin', for sure!" yelled another bitterly.

"'Ere's my tithes and offerin's, Rev'ren' Wesley!" shouted another, and a stone sailed through the air, just missing the little preacher's head.

"My good man, God cares about your troubles and will give you strength in time of—" But the man

named Wesley had to dodge a raw egg that followed the stone. In a few moments, the air was full of shouts and flying missiles—food from lunch pails, eggs on the way to market, even handfuls of mud.

The uproar of the crowd touched Ned's sore feelings. The man had some gall to preach that God loved rich and poor alike! God had never done anything for his family—especially now with Mama sick and Ned laid off work and Papa getting drunk on gin. . . . Ned had a sudden urge to throw the eggs he held in his hand, like the others were doing.

He drew back his left arm and let one fly. It splattered on the preacher's chest. Ned laughed and was just about to throw the next one when he hesitated. Eggs were too precious to waste on a fool preacher, even if it did feel good to hit the mark. Reluctantly, Ned lowered his arm and pushed his way gingerly out of the rowdy crowd.

"Where have you been!" Effie scolded when he came in the cottage door. "That's all Mama needs is another worry!"

"I've been workin'," Ned said curtly, setting the three remaining eggs on the table. "For Mama's breakfast." *And mine, too,* he thought.

Louisa Carter was once again sitting in the chair by the fire, nursing a contented Gilda. She looked better than yesterday, but her face had a stricken look. She didn't even ask him where he got the eggs.

Ned looked around. Effie, Flora, and Dolly were looking at him silently. Wait. Something was wrong. Pip . . . where was Pip?

"Mama!" Ned fell to his knees by his mother's chair. "Where's Pip? Did Papa take him . . . ?" He couldn't choke out the words. He wanted to rip off the stiff bandage around his injured wrist and hit something. It was all his fault! He couldn't work, and now Papa had taken Pip. . . .

Louisa Carter shook her head, her lips trembling. "No, son. He didn't take him to the mines. But . . . he took Pip to try something else—a job better suited for Pip, your father says." Tears slid down his mother's face.

"What do you mean, Mama! What better job?"

His mother laid a hand on Ned's shoulder. "Your father met a man—a merchant in Newcastle—who recruits children to be chimney sweeps for a London firm. He offered your father five pounds outright to train Pip. . . ."

Five pounds! Working all year, Ned and his father and his mother's washing only brought in twenty-five pounds.

"But he can come home each evening, right, Mama?"

Louisa Carter took a trembling breath. "No, that's the trouble of it. Your father says there's no way around it; Pip has to work, what with . . . your injury and my illness. And we agree that Pip isn't suited to the mines. But this merchant says he'll have to send Pip to London—"

"*NO!*" Ned felt the howl come from somewhere deep inside. Not see his little brother again? In all the fears he'd had, he had never imagined Pip just dropping out of his life.

Gilda, startled by Ned's cry, began to wail in her mother's arms. Then Dolly's face puckered and she threw herself in her mother's lap.

Ned scrambled to his feet and stumbled out the

door. He couldn't let this happen! He'd find Pip . . .
they'd run away . . . he'd—he didn't know what he
would do. But he knew one thing: he had to find Pip.

Chapter 5

Found—a Dog
Lost—a Baby

NED HEADED FOR THE RIVERFRONT. What if the man was taking Pip away to London today? If so, they'd probably go by ship; the roads heading south from Newcastle and Gateshead were rocky, rutted things. No carriage or stage coach could get through; only a person on foot or horseback traveled overland in the north of England.

After crossing the bridge, Ned avoided the main road down to the river; he couldn't chance running into his father driving a load of coal to the keel-boats. Instead he scrambled down the bank, stumbling several times because he didn't have his right arm free to keep his balance. Following the river edge he came to the cluster of docks, noisy with shouts, rumbling wagon wheels, and snapping whips.

He ran down the first wooden pier, then the second, then the third, his eyes anxiously searching for a small boy among the boatmen and dock hands. As he worked his way down the busy riverfront, Ned grew more anxious. What if the man and Pip had already ferried out to one of the ships anchored in mid-river . . . or came down the road while he was at the far end of the row of docks? He ran back the way he had come, still scanning the keel-boats tied up at the docks, and almost collided with a team of mules pulling a coal wagon.

"Watch where you're going," the driver yelled, "or you'll break your other arm, you clumsy cockroach!" Ned ducked his head and ran on, hoping the man wouldn't recognize him.

All day Ned watched the docks, but he never saw Pip. When the last keel-boat had pulled away with its load of coal, Ned walked home, his stomach tight with hunger and his shoulders sagging. Was Pip already gone? Would he ever see his brother again?

Then he had a thought. Maybe he didn't find Pip because Pip was still in Newcastle! Maybe the man trained the chimney sweeps here, *then* took them to London. Maybe his brother would come home tonight, and for however many days the training lasted. His hopes renewed, Ned ran the last quarter mile home and burst through the door.

"So! There you are!" Dob Carter said angrily, whirling to face him as Ned stepped into the cottage. "What do you mean ducking out on your mother and staying away all day! Eh? Eh?"

Ned quickly looked around the cottage. His spirit sank. Pip wasn't there. Then he felt his father grab him by the shirt collar.

"I've a mind to give you a thrashing, broken arm or no! Just because you can't drive the coal wagon doesn't give you a right to run around, doing just as you please."

"Dob, please . . ." his mother's voice pleaded.

"I—" Ned was about to defend himself, but he couldn't very well say he'd been looking for Pip all day. His father had decided about Pip, and he'd be angry if Ned interfered.

"I'm sorry, Papa," Ned gulped. "I'll help Mama all I can tomorrow."

Dob Carter released his grip on Ned's shirt. "See that you do," he growled, but the steam seemed to go out of him.   He sat down at the table and drew out a leather bag from his pocket. He poured the coins on the table.

"Here it is, Lou," he said. "Five pounds. It's not much, but it's more than a boy Pip's size could earn in the mines. And it'll be a big help right now, maybe give you some time to get back on your feet."

Ned saw his mother reach out and touch the coins briefly, then pull her hand away. "It's so hard to let him go, Dob . . ." she whispered.

"I know, I know," said her husband. He got up and put his arms around his wife; she leaned into his shoulder. "'Tis just the way it is. It's better than the mines."

But, watching his parents, Ned made a vow to

himself: he'd find Pip—somehow—and bring him home.

✧ ✧ ✧ ✧

The next day Louisa Carter got out of bed, but she still looked pale and sick. Ned tried to help Effie and his younger sisters with the washing. But his clumsy attempts at stirring the clothes in the rinse water, wringing them out, and hanging them up to dry—all with one hand—soon had Effie at her wit's end.

"Mama! Ned is more trouble than help!" she complained, after Ned dropped a nightshirt he'd just help wring out back into the big pot of rinse water. "Can't you give him something else to do?"

Louisa sighed. "Ned, why don't you take Gilda for a walk in the country? The sun is out again . . . she's been cooped up here in the cottage for weeks. That will be a help to me. Here—take some boiled potatoes for lunch."

Ned thought about protesting. He didn't have anything against his baby sister. But he'd been hoping he could deliver a load of dry laundry to a customer in Newcastle; once in town he could ask around about Pip. On second thought, though, this was just as good—maybe better. He hadn't figured out how to carry the heavy basket of laundry with just one arm, anyway. But now he and Gilda could just take a detour into town. . . .

Ned soon discovered, however, that walking with an almost-two-year-old was like walking with a snail.

Gilda stooped to inspect each puddle, waved at every passerby, and simply sat down when she got tired. They got along faster when he carried her on his left hip, but she soon got heavy and he had to put her down again.

When they finally walked through the town gate, Ned realized he had no idea where to start looking for Pip. Newcastle had twenty thousand inhabitants inside the walls— not counting the people who lived across the river in Gateshead or the farmers who brought their food to market. The main street was crowded with people and wagons, and Ned— who normally darted through the streets with little regard for life and limb—was afraid he was going to lose Gilda at any moment.

On an impulse he pulled Gilda into a shop selling fish. "Do you know where they train chimney sweeps?" he asked the shop owner.

"Eh?" said the man, who wore a bloody apron and was busy gutting a fish on his chopping block. He peered at Ned and Gilda beneath shaggy eyebrows. "Chimney sweeps? Heh, heh—you be too big, and she be too little! Ha, ha!" The man laughed at his little joke, and went on gutting fish.

Ned tried another shop—didn't Mama say it was a merchant who took Pip?—but a thin young man just chased them out again. "If you're not here to buy, get away. Go on. Out!"

As they hustled out of the second shop, Ned nearly ran into an older boy who looked familiar. Ned looked again. It was Morgan! The other boy recognized him at about the same time.

"Look where you're going, squirt," Morgan said. Then his eyes took in Ned's bandaged arm and Gilda hanging on his other hand. "Say, heard about your accident. Bad luck."

Ned just glared at him and dragged Gilda down the street. "Hey!" Morgan called after him. "Where's your sister? I haven't seen her for several days."

"None of your business!" Ned snapped over his shoulder. He was glad to hear that Morgan hadn't seen Effie. But how did the town boy hear about the accident if he hadn't seen Effie? Were people talking about him? What were they saying?

His ears red with embarrassment, Ned tried several more shops, but the owners were either too busy to talk to him or they just shrugged and shook their heads.

Discouraged, Ned picked up Gilda with his good arm and trudged back out the town gate. He'd have to come back when he wasn't babysitting if he was going to get anywhere.

Without really paying attention to where he was going, the boy wandered away from the town. Gilda fell asleep on his shoulder, so even though she felt heavy, he just trudged on.

He had walked quite a ways, enjoying the warmth of the sun on his head and neck, when he heard a whimper behind him. Carefully, so as not to wake Gilda, he turned around. A dog was following them. It looked like the same dog he had encountered when he was stealing the eggs the day before—but it was limping and whining pitifully.

Ned looked around. No one was about. Carefully he laid his little sister down in the grass beside the road. She woke slightly, yawned, then burrowed into the grass and closed her eyes again.

Ned turned his attention to the dog. "Here, fella. What happened to your leg?" The dog limped up to him on three legs, tail between its legs and wagging feebly. Ned moved several yards away from the sleeping Gilda so as not to disturb her; the dog followed. He patted the shaggy head, then gently ran his left hand over the dog's body. Several times the dog gave a little yelp, as if he'd touched some sore or injured place. Finally he felt the back leg, which the dog was holding off the ground in an awkward way. The dog growled and snapped at him, then, as if apologetic, licked the boy's hand.

"No blood," mused Ned. "Have you broken a bone, like me, old fella?" He'd been surprised that under the shaggy brown hair, the dog felt bony and ill-fed. Didn't it belong to that farm where he got the eggs? If it was a stray, however, that would explain why the dog didn't raise a fuss when he stole the eggs.

What could he do? He glanced back at Gilda, who lay cuddled in the grass, still asleep. Then he began hunting for sticks that would serve as a splint. The dog limped behind him. He picked up and discarded several sticks—too thin . . . too short . . . too heavy. Finally he found two sticks that were just about the right length and thickness.

Now for a bandage. He untied the strip of cloth around his waist that held the cold potatoes Mama had given him for lunch. He broke one of the potatoes in two and fed half to the dog, who gulped it in two bites, and ate the other half himself. Then Ned tried to splint the little dog's leg.

It was awkward work, given his own broken wrist, and the effort started his arm throbbing painfully. He positioned the two sticks so they stuck out an inch beyond the dog's paw, allowing the dog to rest its leg on the ground without putting any weight on it. It took two or three tries, but the boy finally had the dog's leg splinted.

Suddenly Ned realized a lot of time had passed.

He glanced back down the road, but he couldn't see Gilda! He hadn't realized he had come around a bend, taking him out of sight. He scrambled to his feet and ran back down the road to where he had left his little sister.

But Gilda wasn't there.

He tried not to panic. Surely she couldn't have wandered far. He ran farther down the road, but stopped after a while, sure the little girl couldn't have come this far. He came back to where he'd left her sleeping. Maybe she'd wandered into the bushes and trees off the road. "Gilda! Gilda!" he shouted. Frantically, he checked first the right side of the road, then the left. Still no Gilda.

The limping dog tried to keep up with Ned at first, but finally gave up and just lay down in the middle of the road, its head on its paws, its splinted rear leg sticking out at an odd angle.

After a half hour of frantic searching and calling, Ned was shaking with fright. Gilda was gone. What if someone had come along and taken her? He had to get help—now!

Forgetting everything else, Ned ran back toward town. His legs felt wooden, and he was so scared he could hardly breathe. But he pushed himself on, finally running beside Newcastle's town wall, then over the bridge, and through the narrow streets of Gateshead to the cottage.

"Effie! Where's Mama!" he said hoarsely.

"On the bed—resting," said his older sister. "Why? What's—"

Ned ran into the bedroom. "Gilda . . . lost . . . can't find her!" he blurted out. Without a word Louisa Carter grabbed her shawl and was soon hurrying back down the narrow street toward the bridge with Ned.

Ned tried to tell his mother what had happened. She said nothing, just held onto his good arm grimly, and walked as fast as she could. Over the bridge, past the town gate, out beyond the town. Several times Louisa Carter had to stop and get her breath. Ned noticed that she was shivering, even in the warm afternoon sun, and her forehead was beaded with sweat. He wanted to cry, to beg her forgiveness, but all he could do was walk numbly beside her.

Mother and son finally reached the place where Gilda had been sleeping in the grass. The sick woman's breath was coming hard. "Now . . . tell me . . . where you've looked."

Just then Ned heard a yelp and a bark. He looked back down the road. The shaggy dog with the splinted leg was standing in the middle of the road barking. A

surge of anger rose in Ned's throat. This wouldn't have happened if it hadn't been for that stupid mutt! He grabbed a rock from the rough road and drew back his arm to throw it at the dog.

Then he saw Gilda.

The baby was toddling happily toward the barking dog, waving both her hands in the air like a fat butterfly. How could she be behind them? How had they passed her by?

The dog's barking increased. And that's when Ned saw the horse and rider coming at a trot from the town. The horse had just come around a bend and was almost on top of the little girl. The rider seemed to be sleeping in the saddle—no, he was reading a book!

Ned tried to shout, but the sound stuck in his throat. The dog, however, rushed toward the horse as fast as it could on three legs, barking furiously. Just as the horse reached the baby, the dog leaped up at its nose. Startled, the horse reared up, frightened Gilda beneath its hooves.

Just then, Louisa Carter gave a little moan and collapsed at the side of the road.

Chapter 6

Empty Pocket

NED FELT FROZEN in his tracks. As if in a dream, he saw the horse reel to the side; the book went flying into the air. The rider leaped out of the saddle and swooped up Gilda, whose mouth was now shaped in a big O and wailing loudly. Only then did Ned drop to his knees beside his fallen mother.

"Mama! Mama! It's all right."

But Louisa Carter had fainted.

Ned cradled her head and shoulders in his lap and looked imploringly at the rider who was walking toward them with little Gilda in his arms. The man looked quite shaken himself. As he came closer, Ned recognized the clean-shaven face and long brown hair: it was the strange little preacher from outside the town gate!

"My dear young fellow!" the man said. Ned was again surprised by what a booming voice came out of such a short person. "We nearly had a terrible mishap here. Is this your little sister?"

Ned nodded, suddenly wary. Papa didn't think much of preachers. What was the man going to do?

"Well, I think she is all right, though frightened, I'm sure," the man said. "Now, now, what have we here?" He set Gilda down and bent over Mrs. Carter's limp form. He felt for her pulse, then pried open an eyelid.

"She fainted," Ned said awkwardly.

"I see. Yes, she had quite a fright. But your mother—she is your mother?—is also quite ill with the fever. Catch my horse, will you, lad? I may be able to help her a bit."

Ned reluctantly surrendered his mother to the

man's care and went after the horse who was meekly pulling grass at the side of the road. When he brought the horse back, the man quickly untied a woolen bundle from behind the saddle and placed it under Louisa Carter's head. Her eyes fluttered open and darted in bewilderment from the man to Ned and back to the man.

"Easy, now, my good lady," the man soothed. "Your little one is quite safe. It is you I am concerned about." He fetched a bottle from his saddlebag, pulled out the stopper and tilted the bottle to the sick woman's lips. She swallowed twice and he nodded in satisfaction.

Ned frowned. Who was this man? He'd seen him preaching outside the town gate twice, but he had medicine like a doctor. Whichever he was, he was a stranger, and Ned wasn't eager about letting him doctor his mother. Then he realized that the man was helping his mother sit up and beckoning to Ned to bring Gilda, still snuffling and hiccupping, over to her mother's arms.

"There, now, see? The child is all right. Allow me to introduce myself," the man said. "I am John Wesley of the Methodist Society and I was just leaving Newcastle to preach the Gospel in towns to the north, on my way to Wales. But I am in no hurry. I think this little meeting calls for a picnic."

In amazement, Ned watched as the man un-hooked his saddlebags, and unceremoniously dumped out its contents. Upon seeing the food, Ned suddenly realized he was famished. All he'd eaten since breakfast was half a cold potato—and little Gilda had not even had that!

"Here is some fresh bread—baked yesterday by the good sister at the Orphan House in Newcastle," said the man, passing the bread around cheerfully. "And here is some cheese . . . and cold sausage. Eat hearty, my good people."

"You are kind, sir," Mrs. Carter protested weakly, "but I think this is fare for your travel."

"What does it matter? We shall eat what God provides. And how much better food tastes with good company!"

Ned stuffed some of the sausage in his mouth— oh, how good it tasted! His mother could not seem to eat much, but she broke off pieces of the bread and cheese for Gilda. She also drank gratefully from a flask of water that Mr. Wesley offered.

As Ned filled his stomach with the tasty bread, sausage, and cheese, he felt a nudge on his shoulder. It was the dog with the broken leg. Ned looked at the last piece of sausage in his hand and hesitated. Then he held it out to the dog, who gulped it gratefully. "Guess this has been a rough day for you, too, you mangy mutt," he said grudgingly.

After his hunger was satisfied, Ned wondered how he was going to get his mother home in her shaky condition. But without a word, Mr. Wesley helped Louisa Carter onto his horse and lifted Gilda into the saddle in front of her.

"Oh, my, where is my book?" the little man said suddenly. Ned helped him search in the grass beside the road where the horse had reared and soon found it, somewhat worse for wear but still in one piece.

"Shakespeare," the preacher smiled sheepishly, tucking the book into the now empty saddlebags. "I am on the road so much, it is the only time I get for reading. Lucy, here," and he gave the homely horse an affectionate pat, "usually finds my way for me. Do you read, lad?"

Ned shook his head. "I don't know how to read, sir. Been working the mines since I was five."

"Hmm. A shame. I wonder. . . ." But he didn't say any more.

The strange little group—Ned and Mr. Wesley on foot leading the horse with Mrs. Carter and Gilda, and the dog limping slowly behind—set off down the badly rutted road toward Newcastle.

"You look as though you have had some trouble yourself, lad. What has happened to your arm?"

Without really intending to, Ned found himself telling the preacher about the coal wagon getting stuck in the mud, breaking his wrist and not being able to work, and his little brother Pip now having to work as a chimney sweep. The man was a good listener and said little until they arrived back at the Carter cottage.

Effie came flying out of the cottage, her face red and puffy as though she had been crying. "Oh, Mama . . . Gilda!" she cried.

"Now, now, all is well," soothed Mr. Wesley. "Help your mother to bed, like a good girl. And here—give her two spoonfuls of this medicine three times a day until the bottle is empty."

As Effie bundled their mother into the bed in the smaller room, Ned tried to thank Mr. Wesley for the medicine. "Are you a doctor?" he asked.

Mr. Wesley smiled. "No, but I find I must sometimes minister to the bodies of my flock, as well as their souls. I have read a great deal about medicine; the bottle I gave your mother is one of my own concoctions for cases of fever. Don't worry; it is quite safe and will do her some good."

Effie appeared in the bedroom door. "My mother wishes to thank you."

Mr. Wesley stepped into the little room, but held up his hand when Louisa Carter tried to speak. "Don't trouble yourself to speak, Mrs. Carter. But I have something to say to you and your children." He winked at Flora, Dolly, and Gilda, who were peeking around Effie and Ned and staring at the stranger with open mouths.

"My food and medicine I gladly share. We must care for our bodies so that we can do the work God has given us to do. But, even more important than feeding the body, you must feed your soul. If you have thanks for the food and medicine which I have shared with you, then do me a great favor."

With that, Mr. Wesley told the Carters about the Methodist Society, located at the Orphan House in Newcastle near the Pilgrim Gate. "Good people like yourself meet there to study the Bible and sing praises to God. A lovely lady oversees the Orphan House—Grace Murray is her name. She will welcome you gladly. She organizes classes for women; and we hope to start a reading class for the children, so they can read the Scriptures for themselves." John Wesley glanced at Ned, then turned back to Mrs. Carter. "I beg you—go there on a Sunday, as soon as you are able, dear lady, and receive nourishment for your soul."

Mrs. Carter nodded solemnly, her hair damp against the pillow. "But why must you leave? You are a clergyman. Do you have a church? Is Newcastle your parish?"

Mr. Wesley smiled. "The world is my parish! My church is the open air. Wherever the people are— there I preach."

❖ ❖ ❖ ❖

After the clattering hoofbeats of John Wesley's horse had faded in the direction of the bridge, Effie whirled on Ned.

"Tell me what happened! How did you lose Gilda? What happened to Mama? Where did that man come from?"

Neg tried to ignore her. He felt stupid enough losing Gilda without telling Effie about it. But the girls had seen the dog with the broken leg when Reverend Wesley brought their mother and Gilda home, so the story finally came out. The younger girls immediately declared that the dog was a hero.

"The dog kept the horse from trampling on Gilda!" Flora pointed out.

"Let's keep the doggie! We could call him Hero," begged Dolly.

Ned smiled. That was a good name for the dog.

"Hush!" Effie ordered. "We barely have enough food to feed seven mouths as it is. Do you think Papa would let us take food away from our table to feed a stray dog?"

Ned's smile faded. His sister was right. He didn't dare ask about keeping the dog. Besides, it had probably wandered away by now, anyway.

Afternoon clouds had gathered and twilight quickly filled the narrow alleys of Gateshead. Mrs. Carter slept; Ned helped Flora fold the dry laundry for Mama's customer while Ellie made supper. Suppertime came, but Dob Carter didn't appear. Ellie cast a worried look at Ned, but he shook his head. "Papa doesn't usually drink during the week," he assured her.

The five young Carters had just finished their meal—potato soup again, thinner than usual, and the rest of the barley bread—when Mr. Carter flung open the door and stomped inside.

"Get! Get!" he yelled back into the darkness, then slammed the door shut. "What's that fool dog doing hanging around our door?" he growled. "Never saw such a sight—hopping around on three legs and whining like he belongs here."

Ned gave a start. The dog was still here? He wanted to go outside, but decided he better wait.

Dob Carter smelled strongly of gin, and Ned's heart sank. That was a bad sign. Dob Carter liked his gin, but he was a working man and didn't usually drink with the other men until Saturday night. Even then he usually stopped short of getting drunk . . . except last Saturday night, and a few other times Ned could remember. When things got really bad, that's when his father drank.

"Where's my supper? Where's Lou?" the big man demanded.

"Mama's sleeping—she got sick again," Effie said, quickly placing the lukewarm bowl of soup in front of her father. Her voice was terse and quiet, but Ned could see sparks in her eyes.

Just then Louisa Carter appeared in the doorway, steadied herself, then came and sat at the table with her husband.

Worry lines wrinkled her pale face. "Dob, you've been drinking."

"So? What if I have? A man's entitled to a little pleasure after working all day hauling coal out of that stinking mine."

"But the money, Dob. We can't afford—"

Mr. Carter burst out laughing, but it was a hollow sound. "Money? What money?" And then the laughter turned into a racking sound, and suddenly the big man's head sank into his hands as his elbows rested on the table, and his shoulders shook with dry soundless sobs.

"Dob? Dob? What is it?"

Ned and his sisters watched silently from various corners of the small cottage. What was the matter with their father?

Finally Mr. Carter took a deep breath and shook his head. "I only stopped for one or two drinks, Lou. Things just look so bad, with you being sick and Ned hurt, and putting the little 'un to work. And that's all I had—a couple shots of gin. But . . . when I went to pay . . . that's when I discovered it."

"Discovered what? Dob, tell me what's wrong!"

Dob Carter took another deep breath. "The money— the five pounds that Mister . . . the merchant gave me for Pip. It's gone! Someone stole it right out of my pocket!"

Chapter 7

Runner for Hire

No ONE SPOKE. The children just stared at their parents. The money was gone? What did this mean? The look on their mother's face was frightening. The last bit of color had drained out of it; her lips looked bloodless and her eyes seemed glazed—like a ghost. In a moment she simply rose without a word and went back into the bedroom. A little while later Ned could hear muffled crying.

Later, when everyone had gone to bed, Ned stole noiselessly out of the cottage and sat on the front stoop. In a few moments a shaggy head nosed his arm and gave a little whimper.

Ned fed the dog a crust of bread he'd managed to hide in his shirt. But his mind really wasn't on the dog. His feelings flopped around inside his gut: hot flashes of anger alternated with helpless despair. How could his father be so stupid, carrying all that money around? Even worse was Pip's fate. His five-year-old brother had been hired out as a chimney sweep—but for what? *For nothing!*

It had been a terrible day. His injured hand left him feeling clumsy and powerless . . . he wasn't much help to his mother . . . he didn't know where to look for Pip . . . he had lost Gilda and frightened his mother half to death . . . and now this.

And yet, for a little while—after Gilda had been found and that preacher was so kind to his mother—Ned had felt a flicker of . . . what? Something bright: Hope? Not so discouraged? He wasn't sure what. Mr. Wesley had talked so easily about God, as if there was Someone who cared about them. But now . . . it couldn't be true. His world was crashing in again. The kind man was gone; his brother was gone; the money was gone.

Hot angry tears stung his eyes. The dog licked his face. Wearily Ned pulled the dog close and buried his head in the shaggy hair.

❖ ❖ ❖ ❖

No one mentioned the stolen five pounds again. But Dob Carter came home late from work several days in a row smelling of gin, and when he was home, he just sat staring into the fire. And often Ned heard his mother crying in the bedroom.

Ned was sent to tell certain customers that Mrs. Carter was ill and could not do their laundry this week. "Next week for sure!" he promised hopefully. Back home, Effie and Ned and Flora tried hard to finish the loads that had already been promised, but the work took longer without their mother's expertise and supervision.

Ned didn't dare ask about keeping the dog, but the dog seemed to have made its own decision. Whenever Ned came out of the cottage, the dog soon appeared from somewhere and followed him, hopping along briskly on its three legs. "Hello, Hero," Ned grinned, bestowing Dolly's name on the shaggy creature. Whenever he could, Ned placed food scraps outside the cottage door; the next morning they were always gone.

On Saturday, after receiving his wages of ten shillings and a sack of coal, Dob Carter came home with several sacks of food: oatmeal, barley, potatoes, some salt and sugar, and a little bit of tea. "This will have to do," he said brusquely. Then he sat glumly staring into the fire. Ned knew what he was thinking. The rent came due in a week, and then it would be a choice between food and a roof over their heads.

There was one bright spot in the week, though. The medicine that Reverend Wesley had given Mrs. Carter did wonders, and after several days rest she was greatly improved. On Saturday evening she announced, "Tomorrow I am going to the Methodist Society. I promised Reverend Wesley that I would; it's the least I can do to show my gratefulness for his kindness." She looked around at her family as if to ask, Who will go with me?

Effie snorted. "If you're going to go to church, at least go to the regular Church of England—not some poor people's church that meets in an *Orphan* House."

"Humph," declared Dob Carter. "I grant that Mister Wesley did a kindness, giving you that medicine. And I'm mighty glad you're up and perky again. But he can have his religion. It's not for folks like us. Pious poppycock, if you ask me!" Then he saw the hurt look in his wife's face and shrugged. "But you go if it'll make you happy, Lou."

Ned also shook his head no. In this he agreed with his father. Reverend Wesley was a nice man, but if there was a God, He didn't seem to care much for folks like the Carters.

When Mrs. Carter returned from the Methodist Society Sunday afternoon with Flora, Dolly, and Gilda, she was humming a little tune. Ned and his father looked at each other. The tune was a popular ditty often heard in the pubs along the riverfront. The Methodist Society was a strange "church" if it sang drinking songs! But a little later Ned heard his mother singing some words to the familiar tune as she rocked Gilda:

Jesus, Lover of my soul,
Let me to Thy bosom fly . . .
Hide me, O my Savior, hide,
Till the storm of life is past . . .

Louisa Carter saw him staring at her. "Those words were written by Charles Wesley—John Wesley's brother," she explained. "He's a songwriter. 'Why should the devil have all the good tunes!' he said—at least, that's what they told me at the Methodist Society. And I met the nicest lady. Her name is Grace Murray, just like Reverend Wesley said. She's a widow and lives at the Orphan House. The traveling preachers stay there, and she cooks for them and cares for some of the orphans they take in. And," she said, a bit wistfully, "she invited me to a women's class on Wednesdays."

Ned realized how rarely his mother got away from the cottage, busy as she was with laundry customers, cooking, and caring for children. "You should go, Mama!" he urged.

"Well, I don't know . . . there's so much work to catch up. We'll see."

On Monday it had been a week and two days since Ned had broken his wrist. His mother cut off the old bandage. Oh, that felt good! Ned scratched the itchy skin, but winced when he touched the tender area around the break. Then he stretched out his arm. "Mama, it doesn't look right." The wrist seemed slightly bent at an odd angle.

His mother frowned and examined the wrist carefully. "I'm afraid the bone is not setting straight. Oh, Ned—we should have taken you to a doctor and gotten it set properly."

Ned jerked his arm away. "We didn't have the money, Mama, and you know it," he said tersely. But he felt scared. Would his wrist always be crooked?

He submitted to having the arm wrapped again in the wet poultice which would dry and make a new stiff bandage, but he rejected the sling. "Don't need it," he snapped. Then he blurted something he'd been thinking about. "Mama, I'm no good helping with the laundry with just one hand. I'm going to go to the docks and see if I can find odd jobs running errands or something. I don't need two hands to carry messages."

With his mother's nod, Ned headed for the docks. As usual, Hero appeared out of nowhere and trotted along beside him with his funny three-legged gait. "Hope *your* leg doesn't set crooked," Ned said, a touch of bitterness in his voice.

The boy and the dog wandered among the docks. Besides coal, the docks were the lifeline linking Newcastle and the other northern towns with London and the south. All sorts of goods were being loaded and unloaded into the keel-boats and ferried between the docks and the three-masted ships anchored in deeper water.

"Can you use a messenger?" he asked first this ferryman, then another. "Runner for hire!" he called.

Ned worked his way all down the line of docks, with no luck. But new keel-boats were going out and coming in all the time, so he kept trying. At the same time, Ned tried to keep his eyes and ears open for anything that might give him a clue about chimney sweeps going to London.

The noon hour had passed when his luck changed.

"Hey, boy!" called out a burly ferryman. Ned ran over to him. The man had stripped off his jacket and shirt, and stood sweat-stained and muscular in a dirty undershirt. Ned recognized many of the ferryman who helped unload the coal wagons, but he'd never seen this man before.

"I see you and the dog ha' been in a fight," the man grinned, showing two missing teeth above his scraggly beard. "Looks like you both lost. Ha, ha!"

Ned reddened but said nothing.

"Looking for a job, eh, boy?" the man continued. Ned nodded. "I could use a runner. But I need a boy who can keep his mouth shut about where he's been and what he's carrying. Are you that boy?"

"That I am!" Ned said eagerly. "I'll say nothing but what I'm told."

"Good lad. Now then, I want you to take this packet to the Hogs Head Inn on Iron Alley and ask for a Mr. Driver. Tell him Mr. Harris sent you and give him this packet."

"Yes sir, Mr. Harris." Ned took the packet, stuffed it safely inside his shirt, and started off. Then he turned back to the ferryman. "How shall I be paid, sir?"

The man laughed and tossed him a sixpence. "Return within the hour with a slip signed by Mr. Driver and I'll give you another sixpence."

Ned stared at the sixpence. *Two* sixpence! A whole shilling for just delivering a little packet! Excited, he took off at a run down the line of piers. Avoiding the main road leading up to the town gate from the docks, he scrambled up the steep riverbank, darted between farm carts and coal wagons on the upper road and let the crowd of farmers and market-goers carry him into the town. Hero gamely hopped behind him.

Newcastle had two main streets criss-crossing the town; a web of alleyways filled in the rest of the town within the walls. Iron Alley turned out to be at the far end of town, but as Ned trotted down the narrow passageway, he saw a huge sign with a hogs head painted on it. Even though he couldn't read the words, Ned was confident this was the Hogs Head Inn.

Within a few minutes he had found the man named Mr. Driver, delivered the packet, and was heading back to the town gate. As he turned into the main street, he saw two familiar figures coming toward him: Effie and that Morgan kid! The older boy was helping Effie carry a large laundry basket as Effie chatted. Ned ducked behind a farmer's cart; they hadn't seen him.

So. She was still sneaking around with Morgan. He had been suspicious when Effie said, "No, I can take it myself," every time he offered to help her deliver the baskets to Mama's customers. Now his suspicions were confirmed.

He watched as his sister and Morgan turned

down an alley. Now was his chance to follow them and see where they went! Then he remembered the signed slip of paper he held in his hand: Mr. Harris had said to be back within the hour if he wanted the other sixpence.

Frustrated, Ned let the couple slip out of his sight and headed back toward the docks. True to his word, the ferryman looked at the signed paper and gave him another sixpence.

"Good lad. If you're here tomorrow, you might earn yourself another shilling. Now be off. And remember, where you've been and who you've seen is no one's business but mine."

Ned worked his way back down the docks, still calling, "Runner for hire! Need a messenger?" He was hailed once more, and sent running into the town to buy a loaf of bread and a jug of cider. The smell of the fresh bread made Ned's empty stomach ache. Checking to be sure the baker wasn't looking, Ned slipped a small roll into his shirt on his way out the door, then took a bite as soon as he was out of sight. Oh! It was so light and sweet—not like the heavy barley bread they made at home. Carrying the jug in his good hand and tucking the loaf under his other arm, Ned hurried back to the docks and received twopence for his trouble.

As he headed home at the end of the day, Ned was pleased with the money he'd earned. Over a shilling in one day! It was more than his parents would expect . . . and that's when the idea began to take shape in Ned's mind.

Could he keep aside some of the money he earned and not tell anyone? At this rate, how long would it take him to earn five pounds? He figured quickly: twelvepence to the shilling, twenty shillings to a pound . . . hmm, it would take awhile. But if he could save five pounds, maybe the merchant could be persuaded to let Pip return home.

Back home he laid one sixpence and the twopence on the table. Louisa Carter looked at him in surprise. "Your father will be pleased. God bless you, son."

Ned nodded and turned away. He felt a little guilty but didn't say anything about the other sixpence tied in a corner of his handkerchief in his jacket pocket.

Chapter 8

The Clue

EVERY DAY THAT WEEK Ned returned to the docks. Some days he only picked up one job as a runner; other days he had three or four. He especially liked being a runner for Mr. Harris. The burly ferryman paid him three or four times what the other boatmen paid him to run errands. He always reminded Ned to keep his mouth shut, but Ned didn't mind. What did he care about Mr. Harris' business, as long as he got paid?

Twice more he saw Effie walking with Morgan in the town as she delivered baskets of clean laundry. Once they saw him and Hero; Effie leaned close to Morgan and said something in his ear. Then they looked in his direction and laughed.

"Why were you and that monkey laughing at me

today?" he demanded later that evening.

Effie grinned. "You and that three-legged dog make quite a pair—like two war victims."

"Yeah? Well, I'm going to tell Mama you're running around with a boy behind her back—when you're supposed to be delivering laundry to her customers."

"Go ahead, tattletale. I'm sure Papa would be glad to know about the food you're sneaking to feed a stray dog. Besides, Morgan's mother *is* one of Mama's customers."

Ned glared at his older sister. So that was the way it was going to be, was it? Well, those two weren't going to get away with laughing at him. But he was taken aback to learn that the Carters did laundry for Morgan's family.

By the end of the week Ned had given his parents three shillings, and he had two shillings secretly tied in the handkerchief. Dob Carter was pleased. "Well done, Ned. If you keep at it, you might be able to make almost as much as your wages at the mine."

Ned nodded guiltily. Counting the money in the handkerchief, he'd already earned as much as he earned driving the coal wagon: five shillings a week. But it gave him new determination: he'd work even harder next week and give his family as much as he made at the mine, and keep the rest. Then he wouldn't have to feel guilty about the money that he was saving for Pip.

But it was hard not to feel discouraged. Even though he'd been at the docks all week, he hadn't found out anything about a ship taking chimney sweeps to London.

Breaking into his thoughts, Ned realized his father was still talking to him. ". . . a lot of smuggling goes on at the docks. You watch out. I don't want you running stuff for the black market. Keep your hands clean, you hear?"

On Sunday Mrs. Carter again attended the meeting at the Methodist Society. She came home humming another familiar tune, but again the words were different.

Love divine, all loves excelling,
Joy of heaven, to earth come down . . .

Her husband frowned. "You aren't taking this religion stuff seriously, are you, Lou?"

A little smile lightened Louisa Carter's face. "Oh, Dob, I wish you would come with me. Other workingmen come; everyone's welcome. Somehow hearing God's promises from the Bible and singing praises to Him lifts up my spirit. Our troubles don't seem so heavy; we actually have a lot to be thankful for."

Ned, overhearing, felt like yelling, *No, we don't! Are you forgetting that Pip is lost somewhere between here and London, instead of home where he belongs?* But he held his tongue. No, of course his mother hadn't forgotten. The sad look constantly in her eyes told him that.

Grim and determined, Ned went back to the docks early Monday morning looking for more work. Sev-

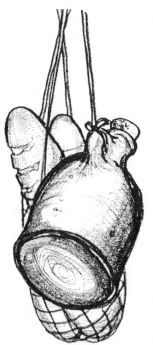

eral times that week he delivered packets or messages for Mr. Harris, and the pay was good. Word also got around that he was quick getting into town to fetch bread and sausage or a jug of cider when the boatmen got hungry. The pay wasn't as good, but Ned was quick to realize that errands to the bakery or farmer's market often netted him an extra roll or hunk of sausage or cheese if he was quick with his hands and took care not to get caught.

He stilled his nagging conscience by telling himself, *If I can eat something in town during the day, I won't have to eat so much at home. And that helps my family.*

One day when he was waiting for Mr. Harris to pay him for a trip to the Hogs Head Inn, he heard someone yell, "Hey, Harris! When is Swift going to deliver on those chimney sweeps we contracted to carry to London?"

"Don't worry about it!" Harris yelled back. "I'm taking care of it."

Ned's scalp prickled. "Mr. Harris!" he blurted. "What did that man mean about chimney—"

"None of your business, boy. Here's your money."

"But, Mr. Harris—!"

"I *said*, none of your business! Didn't I tell you not to ask any questions about what you hear or see? Now, get!"

Ned backed away from the dock, his mind scrambling. The man had said "Swift." Was that the merchant's name who paid his parents for Pip? And what did it mean? Had the chimney sweeps already been taken to London, and the boatmen wanted their money? Or did it mean they were still waiting for this Mr. Swift to deliver the chimney sweeps so they could take them to London? If only he knew!

Impulsively, Ned hurried down the row of docks and up the hill toward town. At least he had a clue. Swift. Swift. He had to find a merchant in Newcastle named Swift. He jostled against someone in his hurry to get into the town gate.

"Hey, don't you ever watch where you're going?"

Startled, Ned looked up into the face of the boy named Morgan. "Get out of my way," Ned snapped.

"Hey, now. You don't have to be so rude. Look, I like your sister; no reason we can't be friendly."

"Oh, yeah?" The last person on earth Ned wanted to talk to right then was Morgan. He wanted to get into town and find Mr. Swift. "There's no reason for you to like my sister. Stick to your own kind, mister, and quit bothering Effie when she's supposed to be working. Now let me by."

Morgan laughed and stood in Ned's way. "Don't be in such a hurry, Ned—that's your name, right? You sure do have a bee under your cap. Say, where's that three-legged dog that's always following you around—oh. There he is. Funny looking mutt, isn't he? What's his name?"

How dare Morgan make fun of Hero! "None of your business," Ned said angrily. "Now, get out of my way!" And without thinking, Ned swung his right fist and connected with Morgan's face.

The pain that shot through his wrist and arm was so sharp that Ned staggered backward and fell against the wall. His arm! His arm! Looking up through watering eyes, he saw blood streaming from Morgan's nose.

"You little beast!" Morgan cried. "I hope you broke your arm again!" The older boy pressed a white handkerchief to his bloody nose and stumbled down the street.

Wagons and people on foot continued to stream

through the town gate, paying little attention to the boy crumpled on the ground against the wall. Ned lay there, breathing hard, until the stabbing pain in his arm eased to a dull throb. Hero lay beside him, giving a small whimper from time to time. Finally, as the boy struggled to his feet, he realized he was in big trouble now.

✧ ✧ ✧ ✧

Somehow Ned staggered home. Tight-lipped, his mother cut off the stiff bandage and made him soak his wrist in cold water to cut down the swelling. Effie looked at him suspiciously, but said nothing. But when Dob Carter got home and heard that Ned had broken his wrist again, he demanded to know how it happened.

Ned looked away from his father's angry face helplessly. He couldn't say it had been a fight over his dog. He wasn't supposed to have a dog.

"A fight, wasn't it?" his father roared. "Otherwise you'd tell me. Two weeks your arm has been healing and now it's broken again! Another six weeks we wait till you can go back to work driving the coal wagon! You idiot! You blasted fool!"

Dob Carter stormed out of the house. Ned saw a pained look on his mother's face. They both knew where he'd end up: at the gin house.

"I'm sorry, Mama," Ned whispered, as his mother once more made the poultice and wrapped his arm. "I didn't mean to make more trouble."

Ned spent a restless night. His arm throbbed and his head ached. Still, he got up early and headed for the docks to continue his bid for odd jobs. But inside Ned felt torn. He wanted to find Mr. Swift. At least now he had a name. But he had to make at least five shillings this week—the same as driving the coal wagon—and hopefully more, so he'd have some to put in the handkerchief. What if he found Pip and didn't have the money to repay Mr. Swift?

But business was slow. It was nearly noon before a ferryman hailed him and sent him to town to deliver a message about some goods that had arrived. The pain in his arm—held tight to his chest once more by a sling—made him feel dull and sluggish. But he delivered the message, received threepence for his trouble, then plodded back through the main street.

Hero, close on Ned's heels as usual, gave a low growl. The boy looked up; a familiar figure was walking ahead of him. It was Morgan. Ned slowed his steps; he didn't want to face the older boy today. As he watched, Morgan went inside a shop. Saddles and harnesses filled the window. Ned looked at the sign which hung overhead. He couldn't read the words, but a saddle was carved into the wood.

Just then two men came out of a baker's shop across the street. "You go on, Jake!" one called to the other. "I've got to pick up my bridle at Swift's Saddle Shop."

Ned was suddenly alert. The man said Swift!

This was it! This was the merchant he'd been looking for!

Chapter 9

Caught

NED WANTED TO DASH across the street and into the saddle shop. But he checked himself; he'd wait until Morgan left. No sense letting that busybody know what he was doing.

Looking up and down the street for a place to wait, Ned was startled to see his sister Effie coming toward him carrying a basket of laundry. Quickly, he ducked into the baker's shop, then peered back out the window. To his amazement, Effie went directly to the saddle shop and entered.

Ned's head was whirling. What did all this mean? First Morgan . . . then Effie. Both of them were in Swift's Saddle Shop—and Swift was the name the ferrymen used when they mentioned taking chimney sweeps to London.

Ned shook his head, as if to sort out the confused thoughts tumbling around in his mind. Effie had said that Morgan's mother was one of Mama's customers. Effie was delivering laundry to Swift's Saddle Shop, and Morgan was there . . . was Morgan the son of Mr. Swift? And if Mr. Swift was the man he was looking for, had his sister known where Pip was all this time and not told him?

Suddenly it all made sense. Mr. Swift heard about Pip from Morgan, and Morgan knew about Pip from Effie. Effie was the connection, and it'd been right under his nose all the time!

Ned felt faint. What was he going to do? His arm throbbed all the way up to his shoulder, and he felt weak with hunger. He looked around; the baker was busy with a customer. A big tray of fresh-baked rolls lay right on the counter by the door. With a quick motion, Ned scooped up two of the rolls, stuck them in his shirt, and stepped out the door.

He had gotten halfway across the street when he heard yelling behind him. Before he knew what was happening, the baker had caught up with him and grabbed him by the jacket collar. "Thief! Thief!" the baker yelled. "I saw you take those rolls. Rob me blind, will you? Give me those rolls!" The baker jerked Ned this way and that.

"My arm!" cried Ned. "You're hurting my arm!"

Rushing up to Ned, Hero barked furiously at the baker.

"Ned! Ned! What's happening?" It was Effie, rushing out of the saddle shop with Morgan close behind.

"I'll tell you what's happening!" sputtered the baker. "This little thief has been stealing bread from me. Take that—!" And he whacked Ned on the side of the head.

A little crowd gathered. "Hang the brat!" someone yelled. "Teach them all a lesson!"

"No!" Effie cried. "Stop! He'll give it back. Stop hitting my brother. He's hurt—can't you see?"

Just then a big voice boomed out, "Here, now, my good fellow. What seems to be the trouble?"

The voice was familiar. Ned squirmed in the baker's grasp, but at first he couldn't see anyone. Then Reverend John Wesley pushed through the crowd and stood before them.

The baker kept his iron grip on Ned's collar. "The trouble is, sir—" the baker huffed, "I caught this here thief stealing my bread. I want my rolls back, and then this boy needs a whipping."

"Or a hanging!" shouted a voice from the crowd.

"You are quite right," said Mr. Wesley calmly, "we must discourage thievery. But I think there must be some misunderstanding. This young man is known to me, and I intend to pay for the bread. Young Master Carter—my bread, please?"

Ned stared at the preacher. What was Mr. Wesley doing back in Newcastle? Then he realized the man was waiting. Slowly he reached inside his shirt and handed the two rolls to Mr. Wesley.

"Now, good baker, what do I owe you?"

The baker looked confused and relaxed his hold on Ned's collar. "Well . . . a ha'penny each."

John Wesley took out a small leather pouch and counted out two pennies. "A penny for the rolls, and a penny for your trouble." Then, smiling at Ned, Mr. Wesley took a big bite of one of the rolls.

Grumbling, the baker went back into his shop and the crowd began to break up. Just then a big man with a thick red beard came out of the saddle shop and pushed his way through the crowd. "What's going on here?" the man demanded. "What do you mean running off like that, Morgan?"

Again Ned stared. This must be Mr. Swift. The saddle merchant had a handsome face, was coatless, and had his shirtsleeves rolled up.

"Uh, Papa, this is Effie's brother," said Morgan, "and . . . er . . . he—"

"So!" the big man said, frowning. "This is the little troublemaker who sent you home with a very bloody nose yesterday."

Effie's eyes widened. "Ned! You didn't!"

Rage boiled up in Ned's chest, and he clenched his left fist. "I did! I did! And if I'd known this rat Morgan told his father about Pip . . . if I'd known his father was the one who took Pip away. . . . I'd . . . I'd have hit him again!"

"Whoa, son," said Mr. Wesley, laying a restraining hand on Ned's shoulder. "What are you talking about?"

Ned pulled away from Wesley's hand and took a step toward Morgan's father. "Are you Mr. Swift? Where's my little brother, Pip Carter? I want to see him right now! You took him away! You stole my brother!"

"Now wait a minute," said Mr. Swift, shaking a finger at Ned. "No one stole anybody. I did your father a favor.

Morgan told me Effie feared that young Pip might be sent to the mines. I have a business contact in London who trains chimney sweeps; he needs little chaps. I sent word through Effie that if your father ever wanted to talk business, to contact me. It was up to him. Couple weeks ago, that's just what he did. Paid him five pounds against Pip's wages."

Ned whirled on Effie. "You *knew*! You knew all the time where Pip was! I've spent weeks looking for him and you knew all the time!"

"But, Ned—!" Effie started.

Ned cut her off and turned a sneering face on Morgan. "Morgan *Swift*. I should have known. I knew from the first day I saw you that you were trouble for the Carters. Just couldn't leave my sister alone, could you? Just couldn't keep your nose out of our business? You . . . you rat! Just wait until my hand heals. I don't care if you are older than I am. I'm going to bloody your face until nobody can recognize you!"

"That's enough!" roared Mr. Swift, his face as red as his beard. "You, sir—what's your name?"

"I am John Wesley, Reverend John Wesley."

"Well, Reverend, you had better take your young friend away, and I don't want to see his face around this saddle shop again. Do you hear, young man? No more threats. You leave Morgan alone, and so help me, if you get in another fight—"

"Quite right, Mr. Swift," said Mr. Wesley quickly, taking Ned by both shoulders and propelling him down the street. "Young Ned, here, needs to calm down, and we need to have a good long talk."

Ned struggled to turn back. "Wait! Wait! I want to see Pip! I want to see my brother, now!"

For a moment everyone froze in silence, broken only by the passersby who were having to go around the little group standing in the middle of the street. Then Mr. Swift cleared his throat.

"I'm afraid that's not possible, young man. Pip Carter was sent to London by ship almost two weeks ago."

Chapter 10

The Orphan House

NED WAS STUNNED. Without a word he let Mr. Wesley lead him away from the saddle shop. He paid no attention to where they were going, and just shook his head when Mr. Wesley offered him the second roll he had bought from the baker.

"Here we are," Mr. Wesley said after a while. "The Orphan House." Ned looked up. The Orphan House was a solid wooden structure of two stories built right against the town wall. A stable was attached. Ned could see Lucy, Mr. Wesley's horse, poking her head out a rough-cut window. Hero wandered over to investigate the stable while Wesley steered the boy inside.

"Mrs. Murray!" the preacher called in his big voice. "A strong cup of tea for my young friend here, please." In a few minutes an attractive woman, her rich brown hair piled on top of her head, came into the front room with a tray of tea and fresh bread and butter. Two young grinning faces peered around the door—boys about eight and ten years old. Mrs. Murray shooed them away and went out, closing the door behind her.

Mr. Wesley poured a big mug of tea with milk and sugar and pushed it at Ned. "Eat and drink, lad. I insist. Then you must tell me what this is all about."

The tea felt good, warming Ned all the way down. Obediently, he buttered a piece of bread. Then, between bites, he told Mr. Wesley everything that had happened since that fateful day when they'd met on the road—everything except the extra shillings tied in the handkerchief.

"So you've been earning money as a runner down at the docks, even with your broken arm . . . good, good." Mr. Wesley nodded approvingly. "That is a good principle, lad. I teach it everywhere. 'Gain all you can'—provided that you do it honestly and don't harm another in the gaining."

Ned squirmed. He suddenly felt uncomfortable about the blind eye and deaf ear he'd agreed to have in running errands for Mr. Harris. His father had warned him about not getting mixed up in the smuggling that went on at the docks. Of course he didn't know *for sure*. But then there was the food he stole nearly every day.

"And all this time you've been looking for your brother Pip, hoping that he was still here in

Newcastle?" Mr. Wesley went on.

Ned nodded.

"A bitter disappointment, lad. Bitter indeed." Mr. Wesley rose and paced about the room, his hands clasped behind his back. "A bad business, taking children from their families. I suppose your father thought it was a better choice than sending the little chap into the mines."

"But it was all for nothing!" Ned said bitterly. "The money Mr. Swift gave Papa was stolen!"

Mr. Wesley stopped pacing and turned to Ned. "But Mr. Swift can't be faulted for that. He gave the money in good faith. Whatever else we may think and feel about this sorry affair, it was a gentleman's agreement between your father and Mr. Swift."

Ned didn't answer. He just felt angry all over again. Mr. Wesley sat down and looked at Ned frankly.

"Now, if you had found Pip here in Newcastle, what were you going to do?"

"Well . . . I . . . I thought if I could save five pounds from my wages, then maybe Mr. Swift would cancel the agreement and let Pip come home."

"Ah! You wanted to redeem your brother!" Mr. Wesley laid a kind hand on Ned's shoulder. "How long would it take to save five pounds, lad?"

Ned thought of the few shillings tied in his handkerchief and shook his head.

"And then what?" Mr. Wesley asked gently. "If your brother came home, would he have to go work in the mines after all?"

"I don't know," Ned said miserably. Then he lifted his eyes to Mr. Wesley's face. "I just know I have to find my brother. I can't just not see him ever again. And Mama—she just hasn't been the same since she let Pip go."

They were interrupted by a light knock and Mrs. Murray stuck her head around the door. "There's a young lady at the door asking after her brother," she said, smiling kindly. She stepped aside and Effie came into the room.

Ned's eyes narrowed and he felt another flush of anger. "How did you find me?"

"Well, Hero's sitting on the front step. That was a big clue," Effie said wryly.

Mr. Wesley greeted Effie with a smile, holding out both hands. "Welcome to the Orphan House, Effie. Come have some tea. You too, Mrs. Murray! Mrs. Murray is our dear hostess and housemother," he explained.

At Effie's quizzical look he chuckled. "The Orphan House is a bit of a misnomer, I admit, since we only have two orphans right now. But the Orphan House is also home to the Methodist Society here in Newcastle."

He turned to Mrs. Murray. "Grace, this is Effie and Ned Carter from Gateshead. I stopped by their house a couple of weeks ago. Maybe you remember me mentioning it."

"Carter?" said Grace Murray, pouring two more mugs of tea for Effie and herself. She had a voice that seemed full of sunshine. "Hasn't your mother been coming to the Society on Sunday for worship? A dear woman. I've been asking her to attend our class for women in midweek, but she hasn't come so far."

Wesley's eyebrows went up. "Mrs. Carter has been attending Sunday service? Good! Good! And now you, Effie and Ned—I would like you to come to our Sunday school. We are teaching the children and young people how to read as well as studying the Holy Book."

Ned shrugged. He couldn't very well say no after Mr. Wesley had come to his rescue a second time. He'd like to learn to read, but . . . nothing seemed very important now that Pip was really gone, and he might never see him again.

As they prepared to leave, Mr. Wesley drew Ned aside. "Ned, don't give up your vow to find your brother. It looks impossible now, but nothing is too hard for God!"

"Even God couldn't find Pip in London without an address," Ned muttered. "And Mr. Swift isn't about to give it to me now."

"Still, you must trust God." Mr. Wesley walked him to the door. "I am staying here in Newcastle for several weeks to train some new leaders, and Mrs. Murray wants my help getting the Sunday school started. Then I shall be traveling once more, this time heading south toward London. In the meantime, will you come to Sunday school?"

Ned shrugged and gave a slight nod.

"Oh, one other thing," said Wesley. "It is wrong to steal food. If you are hungry during the day, come here to the Orphan House and Mrs. Murray will give you something to eat. Do you promise?" Embarrassed, Ned nodded. "Good."

Effie walked Ned as far as the town gate. "I have to pick up some dirty laundry from a customer—but I wanted to talk to you first," Effie said.

Ned was sullen.

"Ned, I didn't know you were looking for Pip. You never told anyone you were. I didn't tell you about Mr. Swift because Papa thought it was best for Mama and the rest of the family not to know who had hired Pip. He knew it would be hard to let Pip go, but once it was done, it couldn't be undone."

"But . . . sent to London, Effie!"

"I know," she said in a small voice. "We were all so

afraid of Pip being hurt or killed in the mines. But—this feels like he's dead."

Her words stabbed him, like ripping off a bandage exposing a raw wound beneath. Yes, that was exactly how it felt—like Pip was dead. Gone. Gone, where they'd never see him again.

Brother and sister arrived at the gate and Ned turned to go down to the docks. The day wasn't over and he needed to get some more work. But Effie stopped him with her hand on his arm.

"Ned, you're wrong about Morgan. He and his father were just trying to help us. I know it feels awful—but just give him a chance."

Ned pulled away and stalked down the road without looking back. He didn't want to even think about Morgan Swift, much less "give him a chance"—whatever that meant. If it hadn't been for Morgan Swift, Pip wouldn't be in London.

Chapter 11

Wesley's Rule

NED HEADED FOR THE DOCKS daily at sunrise, trying to keep himself busy so he didn't have to think. Almost every day he saw John Wesley preaching by the town gate or in the marketplace. Sometimes the crowds were still rowdy, but more people were listening to the little preacher.

By the end of that week, Ned brought home five shillings—same as his wages from driving the coal wagon—and tied another shilling and sixpence in the handkerchief.

He didn't know why he kept saving the money. It would take months to earn five pounds—and a lot of good it was going to do Pip hundreds of miles away in London. But not to do anything felt like giving up. He couldn't just forget about his little brother.

On Sunday afternoon, Effie and Ned appeared with their mother and little sisters at the Orphan House for worship and Sunday school. About thirty men, women, and children were sitting on plain wooden benches. Ned enjoyed the robust singing, led by a man he recognized as another miner. Some of the tunes were familiar, but the words were different. A woman in a homespun dress and cap prayed.

Then John Wesley preached. At first Ned wanted to cover his ears; Mr. Wesley preached as loud in this small room as he did at the town gate! But a few things Wesley said stuck with him: "Are you working for your salvation? It can't be bought. Are you struggling to live holy lives, so you will be good enough to get into heaven? You will never be 'good enough.' Salvation is a free gift from God, available to even the worst sinner. But you have to accept it by faith. *Faith*, brothers and sisters! . . ."

Finally the group sang another hymn and the meeting was over. Then the children and young people were invited into another room for Sunday school. Mr. Wesley began by teaching the alphabet. When they could recognize A, B, C, D, and E, he gave them books and let them pick out these letters. At one point he showed Ned the letters "B," "E" and "D" together.

"That's the word 'BED,' made by putting those letters and sounds together," he explained with a smile.

A sudden spark seemed to light up inside Ned. Maybe he *could* really learn to read! What would it be like to be able to read a book like Mr. Wesley?

The next few weeks seemed to go by in a blur. His father was pleased by the money he was bringing home from running errands at the dock, and Ned could hardly wait for Sunday to learn more of the alphabet and put new words together. His wrist stopped aching and seemed to be healing—though sometimes Ned was afraid that it still didn't look right and might be crooked the rest of his life.

Then one Sunday, Morgan Swift came to the Orphan House on Sunday. Mrs. Carter smiled at him and moved over on the bench to make room for him. Ned smoldered. Was there no end to Morgan Swift? Couldn't they even go to church without Morgan showing up?

The older boy came to Sunday school, too. Ned had a hard time concentrating on the lesson.

"I want you to learn two new words today," Mr. Wesley began. He wrote the words on a large slate with chalk: Y-O-U C-A-N.

"Today," he said, "we are going to learn my 'Rule for Christian Living.' When we come to these two words, read them out loud with me." He held up a large piece of paper with words written on it in black ink.

DO ALL THE GOOD YOU CAN,
BY ALL THE MEANS YOU CAN,
IN ALL THE WAYS YOU CAN,
IN ALL THE PLACES YOU CAN,
AT ALL THE TIMES YOU CAN,
TO ALL THE PEOPLE YOU CAN,
AS LONG AS EVER YOU CAN.

The children repeated the last two words of each line with Mr. Wesley as instructed, and soon were saying the whole "rule" by memory.

After Sunday school, Mr. Wesley motioned for Ned to stay. "So. You are angry that Morgan Swift came today, eh, lad?" he said gently.

Ned hung his head and felt his ears grow red. Could Mr. Wesley see right through him?

"Ned, you will never be able to follow the 'Rule' we learned today as long as there is unforgiveness in your heart. You need to forgive Morgan Swift—and your father, and Effie, and Mr. Smith—for what has happened to Pip. But even more . . ." John Wesley lifted Ned's chin until they were looking eye to eye. "Even more, you need to forgive yourself. I think you are angry at Ned Carter because you broke your wrist. It was an accident that you lost your job at the mine—but deep down you blame yourself."

Mr. Wesley let that sink in. Then he said, "Jesus wants to forgive you whenever you are ready to confess your sins."

Ned said nothing. But all week as he ran errands for the ferrymen at the docks, Mr. Wesley's words burned inside him. *Forgive Morgan? Forgive himself?* All the old feelings he'd been stuffing down by keeping busy and trying not to think about Pip came rushing to the surface. Yes, he was angry! Angry at Effie, and Papa, and Mr. Swift, and Morgan, and . . . and himself. But the anger and pain felt all wrapped around his heart. Would it ever let go?

On Saturday, Ned stopped in at the Orphan House after one of his errands and asked to speak to Mr. Wesley.

He took a deep breath. "I've . . . been thinking about what you said." He swallowed. "I want to . . . to confess my sin and let Jesus forgive me. And . . ." Again he swallowed. ". . . I wish I could forgive Morgan Swift. But, sir, I don't know how."

Mr. Wesley's smile seemed to go from ear to ear. "I'll show you how." And with that, he put his arm around Ned's shoulder and marched him out of the Orphan House and through the streets of Newcastle. Ned was bewildered. Where were they going? A turn here, another there, and suddenly with a sick feeling Ned knew where they were headed.

Swift's Saddle Shop.

Sure enough, the shop soon appeared and Wesley marched right in. He waited until Mr. Swift was through waiting on a customer, then asked to speak to father and son.

The big red-bearded man gave Wesley and Ned a funny look, but went into the back and returned with Morgan. Morgan looked warily at Ned, then at John Wesley.

"Ned has something to say," Mr. Wesley announced.

Ned wanted the floor to open up and swallow him. Say? What was he supposed to say? And then, suddenly, the words were just coming out.

"Morgan, I . . . I'm sorry I hit you and bloodied your nose," he stammered. "I didn't really mean to; it just happened. I was upset and you got in my way. And, uh, I'm sorry for a lot of nasty things I've said, too. Effie says you're not a bad sort. But I've never given you a chance."

There. He had said it. And then he realized the

anger that had been squeezing him inside for weeks seemed to be loosening its grip.

A grin spread over Morgan's face. "That's all right. Guess you hurt yourself worse than you hurt me—breaking your arm again, I mean. And, say, Ned, I know how you feel about Pip. But you've got to believe me, I was just trying to help Effie and your family. Otherwise, it looked like Pip would have to go to the mines—little kid like him."

"I know."

There was an awkward silence. Then Mr. Swift cleared his throat. "Well, now, that was a fine apology, lad. And since you've apologized, I take back what I said about not showing your face around here. You're welcome any time—might even have some errands you could do while your arm is healing."

Ned couldn't believe they were having this conversation. Is this what forgiveness was all about? He looked at Mr. Wesley, but the preacher had a serious, intense look on his face.

"The lad appreciates that, I'm sure, Mr. Swift. But I have another favor to ask you. Would you be so kind as to tell us the name of your business contact in London, the one who trains chimney sweeps, and where he might be located?"

Ned was not the only one who was startled. Mr. Swift was suddenly wary again.

"My intention is not to cause trouble," Mr. Wesley assured the shopkeeper. "My only concern is the welfare of a young boy. There may be some alternatives that would be good for all concerned."

"Hmm." Mr. Swift rubbed his red beard thoughtfully. "I suppose it would be all right. Mr. Timothy Bobbitt is the name. Top Hat Chimney Specialists, Limited. Billingsgate."

John Wesley politely bowed his head. "I thank you. Now good day, and God bless you."

Ned followed Mr. Wesley out of the shop, his mind in a whirl. "Why did you ask him that? What good will that do? London is a couple hundred miles from Newcastle!"

"Quite right, lad, you're quite right. But I have an idea. If only your father will hear me out!"

Chapter 12

The Egg Bath

NED WAS ALERT, wondering what John Wesley was going to do. The small preacher sat at the table in the Carter cottage facing Ned's mother and father.

"God has called me to travel from town to town all over England," Mr. Wesley was saying. "Sometimes I ride more than four thousand miles in one year! I preach wherever the people are, to whoever will listen. I visit and encourage the Methodist Societies wherever they are, and attempt to establish a Society where there is none."

"Are you a regular clergyman, then, or just an impostor?" asked Dob Carter bluntly.

Mr. Wesley smiled. "I am an ordained minister of the Church of England. But God has given me a message of salvation by faith for all the people—and all the people don't attend church."

Dob Carter shifted on the bench uneasily.

"But I'm not a young man any more," Wesley went on, "and these middle-aged bones are starting to protest the long days in the saddle. I've been thinking of hiring a coach—"

Ned's father shook his head. "Won't work. No road going north or south of Newcastle is fit for anything but a man on foot or horseback."

Wesley laughed in agreement. "You are right! Terrible roads. But once one gets to York, the roads are passable. What I need is a coach driver, and I would like to hire Ned."

Louisa Carter gave a small gasp and Ned's mouth dropped open. He could hardly believe what he was hearing.

"Hire Ned?" Dob Carter could hardly believe it either. "The boy has a broken arm, can't even drive a coal wagon! Besides, we can't spare him. We're a poor family, Mr. Wesley, and we need every wage-earner to pull a fair share."

"Exactly," said Wesley. "That's why I'm willing to pay Ned six shillings a week—paid directly to you—plus his expenses while he's with me."

Six shillings a week! That was a shilling more than Ned made working at the mine. Ned could see that his father was considering the idea. But then Dob Carter shook his head again.

"I'm an honest man, Reverend Wesley. So I have to say I don't know whether the boy can do it. Oh, he's a good driver, but it was a bad break, and he broke it again through his tomfoolery. Also . . ." His father avoided Ned's eyes. ". . . we couldn't afford to pay a doctor to set it properly. To put it bluntly, we don't know if the boy's arm is going to be all right even when it's mended."

At his father's words Ned blurted, "Oh, but it will, Papa! It's been four weeks since the second break, and it feels stronger every day. By the time we get to York, I'm sure I'll be able to drive a coach."

John Wesley turned to Mrs. Carter. "I know you are grieving Pip's absence, dear lady, and for that reason I hesitate to take away another son. But I assure you, Ned will return in several months time, when we come this way again."

"Thank you," she said gratefully. "You read my heart."

"There is another reason I wish to take Ned with me," Wesley added. "He has made good progress in learning to read. I was a teacher before I was a preacher, and I would like to continue with Ned's education." He leaned forward toward Mr. Carter. "My good sir, if there is ever to be another future besides the pit mines for the Carter family, it must come through education."

To Ned's astonishment, it was decided: he could go with Mr. Wesley as his coach driver.

✧ ✧ ✧ ✧

Late October was cool and damp as Wesley's horse and the gentle mare borrowed for Ned from the

Orphan House headed south along the muddy road leading away from Newcastle and Gateshead—toward London. Hero, who had long since shed the splint on his hind leg, trotted along behind for awhile with only a slight limp, but three times Ned chased him back toward town. Finally the dog sat forlornly in the middle of the road until the horses were out of sight.

For awhile Ned rode in silence, worried about the dog. Who would take care of Hero now that he was gone? Still, it couldn't be helped. And Ned, who had never been away from the busy port on the Tyne River, grew more excited as the miles slogged away beneath the horses' hooves. But he was curious about something.

"You didn't say anything to my parents about trying to find Pip when we get to London. Why not?"

"Because I don't know what will happen when we get there, and I don't want to raise their hopes. Like Abraham and Isaac, we're just 'going up the mountain in obedience to the word of the Lord.' God will have to provide the sacrificial lamb."

Ned was totally confused. What kind of talk was that? Must be some kind of Bible story. Still, there was another question he wanted to ask, but he waited until they stopped by the side of the road to eat their lunch of barley bread and cheese.

"Sir, you don't seem to have very much money yourself. Your clothes are plain and mended. You once told me to 'Gain all you can.' But you don't do any work—that earns money, I mean," he hastened to add. "How can you pay me wages to be your coach driver?"

Wesley chuckled. "A very good question, indeed. Yes, I said one should 'gain all you can'—provided that you do it honestly and don't harm another in the gaining. But that is only part of what I teach about money."

Ned noticed that Mr. Wesley's voice took on its preaching tone, even if the 'congregation' only consisted of one thirteen-year-old boy and two horses who weren't paying attention.

"My second principle is: 'Save all you can.' Don't waste your earnings on frivolous spending, luxuries and entertainments. Save all you can to take care of your basic needs: simple food, simple shelter, simple clothes. It's healthier in the long run, anyway.

"And that leads to my third principle: 'Give all you can.' God doesn't give us money to hoard it. When basic needs are met, then we must give all we can to those who need it, to the glory of God."

Wesley repacked the food into his saddlebags. "Don't worry, Ned. God has provided for all my needs, and more. The rest I distribute to those who can benefit."

The man and boy remounted and pushed on along the northern English countryside, passing large pastures of woolly sheep, shabby little farms, long rows of stones marking boundaries. They passed the miles in silence.

Ned thought about what John Wesley had said. He certainly had a practical method for everything: be thrifty, eat right, take care of your health, do good to your fellow man, patch up quarrels, forgive your enemies, memorize Scripture . . . suddenly Ned laughed out loud.

"I just figured out what 'Methodist' means," he said, grinning at his startled companion. "You have a method for doing everything—a very practical Christianity!"

Mr. Wesley chuckled. "Blame my mother for that! A more practical woman you never did see than Susannah Wesley. She held our family together by her wits while my father—an altogether impractical man—wrote poetry and championed causes. Although . . . I guess my brother Charles and I are a mixture of the two."

In York, the Methodist Society there had prepared a coach for Wesley's journeys. It had a writing table built inside so that he could study along the way. Ned felt nervous mounting the driver's seat and picking up the reins of the team of horses for the first time since his accident. His wrist felt weak, but Mr. Wesley encouraged him to take it slow, and the first day or two passed without incident—though Ned's arms were tired and aching by the time they pulled into the next town.

Whenever they came to a town, Wesley was ready to preach. But each time a crowd gathered, Ned felt nervous. The people behaved very much like the crowd outside the town gate at Newcastle the first time Ned had seen Wesley preach: yelling, throwing things, laughing at the little man standing on a box or wagon bed or well cover, who was trying to tell them that God loved them, rich and poor alike.

At one mining town, a gentleman in a powdered wig and an expensive coat pushed through the crowd of curious common folk, waving his carved walking stick. "Go home! Don't pay attention to this Methodist devil!" he shouted, cursing heavily. "If you want religion, go to church on Sunday. Now, get back to work, lazy good-for-nothings."

Ned, who was standing nearby holding his coach whip, spoke up. "Sir, if I hear Mr. Wesley right, I don't think God approves of such foul language."

Several people nearby snickered. The gentleman reddened.

"Who are you? Do you think *I* need to be taught by a mere coach boy?"

Ned said politely, "Yes, sir, I do think so. We are all sinners—rich and poor alike—and we all need the Gospel Mr. Wesley preaches."

The man shut his lips in silent fury and pushed his way roughly out of the crowd. When John Wesley heard of it, he shook his head with a funny smile. "I may step down and let you do my preaching, Ned."

The weeks rolled by, one after the other. Ned lost track of the many towns they stopped in. The fall rains were almost daily, now, leaving the roads slippery with mud. At least once a day they had to dig the coach out of the ruts, and several times Ned strained his wrist hauling back on the reins as the two coach horses floundered down a slick hill. Ned's confidence faltered, but Mr. Wesley patiently bound up the boy's wrist to give it added strength, and sometimes they stayed an extra day or two with kind people from one of the Methodist Societies until his wrist felt better.

"London is only a few days away," John Wesley said encouragingly to Ned as he climbed out of the coach at Bedford, about fifty miles north of London. Ned was tired, but he got out the box they carried for Wesley to stand on, and soon Wesley began preaching to the passersby in the dreary drizzle. As usual, a crowd quickly formed, shoving and shouting. Wesley calmly kept preaching, his booming voice cutting through the constant heckling.

Ned saw a man dressed in rough homespun push his way through the crowd, carefully carrying a small sack. Sensing trouble, Ned edged closer to see what he was up to. The man stood at the front, seeming to listen, but Ned saw him transfer several raw eggs from the sack into the pocket of his coat.

Ned knew it would be only moments before Mr. Wesley would be pelted with the eggs—rotten, he guessed. But what could he do? The man was big and husky, built like his father. Then suddenly Ned had an impulse.

"Uncle!" he cried, flinging his arms around the man in a big bear hug. He squeezed hard in his mock embrace.

Then he pulled back and feigned surprise. "Oh! I'm sorry! I mistook you for my uncle I was to meet here today." And Ned quickly melted back into the crowd.

The man was so surprised, it took him a few moments to realize the eggs in his pockets had been crushed. As the rotten smell soaked into his clothes, the crowd fell back, laughing, leaving the man standing alone, mouth gaping in embarrassment.

John Wesley ignored the disturbance and kept right on preaching. Later, however, as they walked through the streets to find lodging, Wesley laid his arm across Ned's shoulders.

"That was a clever trick, Ned, and I appreciate you standing up for me. But I do not fear a few rotten eggs."

Ned grinned sheepishly. "I know. But I once threw an egg at you . . . in Newcastle! . . . I was too embarrassed to tell you. I guess today I just wanted to make amends."

Wesley laughed. "All is forgiven! Come, now, let's have a hot meal, dry our damp clothes, and have a short reading lesson from the Holy Book. Tomorrow at dawn we leave for London!"

Chapter 13

London

LONG BEFORE THEY REACHED LONDON, Ned saw the smoky smudge hanging low on the horizon. As the coach horses clipped along the road, the smudge grew larger until it filled half the sky.

Ned realized he was gripping the reins too hard. A strange tension was building inside him. He took a big breath and tried to relax. The road into the city was crowded with wagons, coaches, and people on foot and horseback, and he had to keep alert to avoid an accident.

Even Newcastle, the largest city in northern England, had not prepared Ned for London. Coal smoke belched from hundreds of chimneys, creating the black cloud which hung low overhead. Horses pulling grand carriages thundered through the streets with little regard for who was in the way. Small, dirty boys and girls darted in and out of the traffic. Men and women pushing carts were trying to sell their wares, yelling hoarsely. The streets were dirty, and a foul smell clung to everything.

Mr. Wesley, who was sitting beside Ned on the driver's seat, pointed toward the River Thames which divided the city, and Ned guided the coach horses along Lower Thames Street until they came to London Bridge. The Tower of London rose harshly behind them as they crossed the bridge. And just like any other London street, this one was crowded with houses, shops, and factories on either side.

Darkness had fallen over the city when Wesley told Ned to pull up beside a large plain building. A large sign was nailed beside the door: "The Foundry."

"This is it, Ned," Wesley said, "the Methodist headquarters! Used to be a cannon factory, but we're putting it to better use. Come, lad, let's go in!"

A meeting was in progress, and the hearty singing filled one of the big factory rooms. As they stood at the door at the back of the meeting, Wesley's booming voice joined in the singing.

> . . . *With th'angelic host proclaim,*
> *"Christ is born in Bethlehem!"*
> *Hark! the herald angels sing,*
> *"Glory to the newborn King."*

Ned was startled by the words. They'd been on the road almost two months, and it was nearly Christmas!

The effect of Wesley's voice on the group in The Foundry was immediate. People turned with glad cries and greetings.

"John!" cried a voice, and a man scrambled over the benches and gave Wesley a big bear hug. "We heard you were coming, but didn't know when."

"Charles!" laughed John Wesley. "It's so good to see you. Ned, this is my brother Charles—the one who is responsible for all the singing we Methodists do! But let's not interrupt this meeting. Let's praise God for bringing us together again."

Someone went out to care for the coach and horses, and the rest took up their joyous singing. The meeting lasted till late, and Ned fell asleep in spite of himself. When he awoke the next morning, he was in a warm bed with a wash basin, pitcher of water, and towel next to it. He quickly washed, and wandered through The Foundry until he found John and Charles Wesley having a simple breakfast, served by two smiling Methodist "sisters."

"Sit down, lad, and eat!" welcomed John. "I have just been telling Charles your story, and our hope of finding your brother Pip here in London. We shall go today to Billingsgate across the Thames River and see if we can locate Mr. Timothy Bobbitt and his Top Hat Chimney Specialists!"

Ned's heart leaped. Just like that? Was it possible that he might find Pip today?

True to his word, John Wesley, his brother Charles, and Ned set out on foot through the narrow streets, crossed London Bridge once more and picked their way through a large market crowded along the river. Ned hunched his shoulders against the chilly wind, then realized it was snowing lightly. The wet flakes melted into the dirty slush as fast as they fell, however.

As they passed through one narrow passageway, a window opened above and a bucket of slop was tossed out onto the pavement, splattering their boots. *Whew!* thought Ned. *That was close.* He didn't want be soaking wet and smelling like a barnyard when he found Pip.

The trio walked up and down the area called Billingsgate, peering at the signs hung on the buildings, and suddenly Charles called out, "Is this what you're looking for?" The sign on the gloomy building said, "T. Bobbitt, Esq. Top Hat Chimney Specialists, Ltd."

Ned's throat was so dry he could hardly swallow as John Wesley banged the large, brass knocker. Several minutes and several knocks later, a pudgy young man wearing spectacles and a waistcoat opened the door.

"Mr. Timothy Bobbitt, if you please? We are here on business," said Mr. Wesley crisply.

"Come along, then," grumbled the young man, who was probably Bobbitt's clerk. He led the way through a narrow hallway, then knocked on an office door.

"Gentlemen to see you, Mr. Bobbitt," he announced in a dull voice, then disappeared behind another door.

John and Charles Wesley and Ned found themselves standing in a stuffy little room, the coal stove in the corner glowing bright red.

"Yes?" said the man behind the desk. Timothy Bobbitt was nearly bald on top, and his chin was bare, but he had big, hairy sideburns and was puffing on a pipe curved like the letter S.

"Mr. Bobbitt? My name is John Wesley, and this is my brother Charles Wesley. We are clergymen, and are here to inquire about one of your chimney sweeps, a lad named Pip Carter."

Mr. Bobbitt frowned and peered at them through narrowed eyes. "What's 'e done?"

Wesley held up his hand. "We are clergymen, not the law, Mr. Bobbitt. This young man," he indicated

Ned, "is the lad's brother. He has come to find his brother Pip and return him to his family in Newcastle."

Ned could hardly breathe in the stifling hot room.

"Nonsense!" said Mr. Bobbitt, taking the pipe out of his teeth and jabbing the mouthpiece at them. "I pay good money to hire my sweeps. What sort of business could I run if I let 'em go, just because somebody back home gets homesick? Besides—I don't know if this 'Pip' you're looking for is even one of my sweeps. I have a hundred lads, and more, scattered around London! This is just the office of Top Hat Chimney Specialists. I have foremen who manage small groups of lads, covering my business in different parts of the city. They keep track of the lads—not me. Now be off. I'm sorry you've come so far for nothing."

To Ned's dismay, John Wesley bowed his head politely and led the way back down the narrow hallway. Out on the front step, with snow swirling around them, Ned faced John Wesley angrily.

"We're not giving up, are we? We're so close! Pip could be nearby this very moment! I—!"

"Easy, lad," Mr. Wesley interrupted, taking Ned's arm, and leading him back the way they had come. "It took Joshua seven days and thirteen trips around Jericho before the walls fell down. Trust in God; it is He who gives the victory. Mr. Bobbitt is only a mere wall in the way of the Lord's army."

It always bewildered Ned when Mr. Wesley talked like that. He didn't know who Joshua was, but he sure liked the idea of the walls around the office of Top Hat Chimney Specialists falling down!

Both John and Charles Wesley were busy the rest of the day with matters relating to the Methodist Society, so Ned spent the day brushing the mud out of the coach horses' manes and tails and cleaning their stalls. But the next day, the two Wesley brothers, Ned, and two other men from the Methodist Society walked once more across London Bridge, past the Billingsgate market, and banged the knocker on the door of Top Hat, Limited.

Mr. Timothy Bobbitt was not pleased to see them. John Wesley stated their request once more, and Mr. Bobbitt, puffing his pipe in annoyance, again refused. To Ned's dismay, the little group retreated once again without argument.

On the third day, however, the group that made its way to the office of Top Hat, Limited, had doubled. This time eight men and women, plus Ned, stood in front of Mr. Timothy Bobbitt's desk.

"Now, see here, Mr. Wesley," Bobbitt sputtered. "What do you mean bringing all these people here? I'm a busy man; you are hindering my business. Be off with you, or I'll call the sheriff."

"Your business is built on the misery of innocent lads, too young to know they are being taken advantage of," said John Wesley, wagging a finger in Mr. Bobbitt's face. "If you wish to be rid of us, release the lad named Pip Carter once again to his brother and family. But we will not be unfair: name your terms."

"Get out! Out!" shouted Mr. Bobbitt.

The group retreated, though at the door John Wesley turned and said calmly, "Call the sheriff if you like; it will only serve to advertise our cause."

On the following day, Ned was amazed to see the group going to Billingsgate had doubled once again—sixteen adults, mostly mothers now, holding babies in their arms and small children by the hand. In front of the Top Hat office, they sang a rousing hymn, drawing curious onlookers. Then the Methodists entered the building and packed Bobbitt's office.

Mr. Bobbitt stood up and faced them coldly. "You want my terms? Ten pounds. You can have the boy for ten pounds, and not a farthing less!"

Ned gasped, his mind a whirl. Mr. Bobbitt was agreeing to release Pip! But—ten pounds! That was several months' wage for a poor man. He thought of the ten shillings he had saved in his handkerchief: only half a pound! A mere drop when he needed a bucketful! Suddenly the hope of claiming Pip, which had flared brightly just seconds before, dimmed.

No one said anything about the ten pounds on the way back to The Foundry, and Ned spent the rest of the day fiercely cleaning the harnesses in the stable. But that evening after supper he asked to speak to John Wesley alone.

The candle on the table flickered bravely in the drafty Foundry as Ned slowly pulled the handkerchief from his jacket pocket, untied the knot, and spilled the coins on the table. "It's not enough, but it's all I have," he said, pushing the words past the lump in his throat. "Oh, Mr. Wesley, what will I do?"

John Wesley stared at the money, then looked at Ned for a long time before he spoke. "That's all God asks of you, Ned—to give all you have," he said gently. "It's never enough, but God takes what we have and works miracles. Trust in God."

Dejected, Ned lay in his bed, tossing and turning. Trust in God? How could God take ten shillings and make it into ten pounds! Everything he ever tried to do was never enough! He couldn't get his coal wagon unstuck without breaking his arm. He couldn't take his little sister for a walk without losing her. He couldn't even slug Morgan Smith in the nose without hurting himself! But worst of all, he couldn't earn enough money to redeem his little brother, even though Mr. Bobbitt was willing to let him go! Hot tears stung his eyes; exhausted, Ned finally fell asleep.

When Ned awoke the next morning, he heard the murmur of many voices, as if a meeting was going on. Pulling on his trousers and boots, he came downstairs into the hall, only to see men and women coming in the door of the Foundry, as others went out.

"Merry Christmas tomorrow!" A plump woman smothered him with a motherly hug before stepping out into the slushy street.

"God bless you, lad," said a man, shaking his hand, then he disappeared into the meeting room.

Ned stood bewildered as people greeted him coming and going. Finally, as the visitors thinned out, Ned peeked into the meeting room.

"Come in, Ned!" boomed John Wesley. "Let's see how God has multiplied your five loaves and two fishes!" The two Wesley brothers were gleefully counting a basket of coins.

". . . five pounds sixpence . . . ah! half a crown! And another . . . and a guinea! . . . that makes six pounds, six shillings and sixpence . . . ."

Ned stared as the two men continued to count. Finally John Wesley looked up. "Nine pounds, fifteen shillings."

"Wait," said his brother. Charles Wesley took out a little pouch from his pocket and emptied the contents into the basket.

"Five more shillings," counted John. "Praise God in heaven! We have ten pounds! Come on, lad—we're going to pay a visit to Mr. Bobbitt!"

✧ ✧ ✧ ✧

Mr. Bobbitt's office was stifling hot, and again Ned found it hard to breathe as the businessman carefully counted the money, not once, but twice. He finally grunted and jerked his head toward his clerk.

"Get the boy."

Only a few minutes went by before Ned heard footsteps in the hall again, but it seemed like hours. The door opened and a small boy stood there, looking frightened and bewildered. His clothes and hair were almost black with soot; an attempt had been made to clean his face and hands, but they, too, were streaked with gray. His round eyes looked at the man puffing sullenly on his pipe behind the desk, then the two men in plain coats standing quietly to the side. Finally his eyes rested on Ned and widened.

Ned wet his lips before he could speak. "Pip! It's me, Ned! I've come to take you home."

For a moment the little boy didn't move. Then with a wild cry he flung himself in Ned's arms.

Chapter 14

Home Again

THAT NIGHT PIP SHARED NED'S BED at The Foundry, just as they did at home. The Methodist ladies had scrubbed the little boy until he squeaked, but his clothes were declared hopeless. Word had gone out among the Society families, and soon a nice bundle of clean, used clothes had been gathered for the little chimney sweep.

As Pip fell asleep, Ned gently loosened Pip's arms, which were wrapped tightly around his neck, so he could breathe. He could hardly believe his brother was snuggled safely beside him. It had only been four months since the accident—four months since Pip had been sent away—but it seemed like four years.

Lying in the darkness, with Pip's slow, even

breathing in his ear, Ned remembered the angry weeks he'd spent trying to find Pip, all the errands he'd run trying to save enough money to redeem his brother. He'd worked so hard, *so hard*, but all his efforts just weren't enough. And yet . . . here was Pip, safe and sound. They were together again! It was like a gift, just handed to him.

Suddenly Ned's eyes flew open. Why, that was what Mr. Wesley had been preaching about all the way from Newcastle to London! Salvation by faith . . . a gift from God . . . God's grace, not by our own efforts. . . .

Ned was wide awake. Slipping out of the bed so as not to wake Pip, he pulled on his trousers and tiptoed into the hall. He saw a faint light under Mr. Wesley's door and knocked lightly.

"Come in."

Ned opened the door and peered in. John Wesley was reading his Bible with the aid of a candle. But when he saw Ned he beckoned the boy to come in. "Is something troubling you, lad?" he said kindly.

Ned sat on the edge of the bed. "No. It's just that I understand now."

"Oh?" Mr. Wesley raised his eyebrows.

"I wanted to save Pip," Ned blurted, "but no matter how hard I tried, I couldn't do it by myself. But you and the others in the Methodist Society, you redeemed Pip! You didn't do it for yourselves, you did it for me."

A smile flickered at the corners of Wesley's mouth. "Yes, go on."

"That's just like Jesus, isn't it? I mean, He redeemed us on the cross. You keep saying salvation is a free gift."

Wesley nodded. "That's right. We have to accept God's gift, or it does us no good. We have to believe."

Ned took a big breath. "Well, I just wanted to tell you . . . I believe."

John Wesley threw back his head with a joyful laugh. "Hallelujah!" he shouted, forgetting that people were asleep.

Just then they heard church bells begin to ring in the darkness outside. Boing, bong . . . boing, bong. On and on they went.

Mr. Wesley gave Ned a wide smile. "It's midnight—Christmas Day. Merry Christmas, Ned. Christ is born in your heart today!"

A few minutes later Ned crawled under the blankets beside Pip. Christ in his heart . . . Pip safe in the bed. It was the very best Christmas he'd ever had.

✧ ✧ ✧ ✧

Spring had flowered in northern England when Wesley's horse and the Orphan House mare once again picked their way over the rutted, rocky roads. The travelers had left their coach in York, and with Pip riding behind Ned, they were pushing on toward Newcastle-upon-Tyne.

"Don't hold so tight, Pip," Ned scolded.

But Pip in his excitement didn't seem to hear. "Are we going to get home today, Ned? You said today. Look! I saw a bunny under that bush. There—there! Did you see it, Ned? It was a gray bunny. . . ." On and on the little boy chattered.

Ned sighed. For months he had dreamed about this day when they would return to Newcastle. But now that they were almost there, he began to worry. What would happen when they got home? Would Pip have to work in the mines after all? And what would he do? Mr. Wesley was traveling on toward Scotland, where the roads were just as bad as northern England, if not worse. The preacher wouldn't need a coach driver now—at least not for awhile.

But could he drive the coal wagons yet? Ned stretched out his arm and examined his wrist, which had set slightly crooked. He managed all right most of the time, but heavy strain often left his arm sore and shaking.

He glanced at Mr. Wesley, who was absorbed in a book, letting Lucy, his horse, choose the best footing along the rough road. Last night Ned had mentioned his worries to the preacher, and Wesley had said what he always said: "Trust in God, Ned."

But in spite of his worries, Ned's excitement grew as they rode into Gateshead, wound their way through the narrow streets, and pulled up in front of the Carter cottage. In a flash, Pip slid off the mare's back and ran inside. Immediately there were surprised cries and squeals of joy.

The next hour seemed like a blur, with everyone hugging and talking at once. But finally Dob Carter had come home from work, supper was placed on the table, and the eight Carters and John Wesley squeezed together on the benches around the table. To Ned's surprise, his father didn't plunge his spoon into the big bowl of mutton stew in the center of the table, but instead the whole family held hands around the table and began to sing:

Be present at our table, Lord,
Be here and everywhere adored;
These mercies bless and grant that we
May feast in paradise with thee.

John Wesley was grinning from ear to ear. Ned blurted out, "That's Charles Wesley's table grace!"

Dob Carter cleared his throat. "Well, yes. We also have a story or two to tell." Dolly and Flora giggled behind their hands, but Louisa Carter just encouraged her husband with a smile.

"Well, you see, Louisa, here, kept after me to attend the meetings of the Methodist Society on Sundays. Finally, just to keep peace in the family, I went with her and the girls. I'd never attended church before—always thought religion was for rich folks. Ned knows my thoughts on that."

Ned grinned.

"Well, most of the folks were working people like ourselves. Mrs. Murray was very kind to my wife, and I could see a change in her spirit. So I kept going back, and the preaching began to sink in. To make a long story short, you see a new man sitting before you this day. And ever since I asked God to save me, I haven't touched a drop of gin. Not that I haven't been tempted! But God's power is stronger than my feeble will."

Mr. Wesley threw up his hands. "Praise God! Salvation has come to this household."

And then the hubbub began, as the stories of the journey to London, the Methodist Societies' headquarters at The Foundry, and Pip's redemption were told all over again.

Before Mr. Wesley left that night to go to the Orphan House, he laid a hand on Ned's shoulder. "You have a way with horses, lad. We need a boy at the Orphan House to take care of the post horses that we keep there for the traveling preachers who need a fresh mount. It's not a full time job, but talk it over with your father. And, remember, trust in God."

The next morning Dob Carter shook Ned awake by the shoulder. "Come, lad," he whispered. "We have some business to take care of."

Obediently Ned got up quietly, so as not to disturb Pip, ate the familiar oatmeal, and followed his father through the streets of Gateshead. He had a feeling of dread as they crossed the bridge to Newcastle. Were they going to the mines?

But instead of taking the road past the town, Dob Carter led Ned through the town gate and threaded their way through the early morning crowd. To Ned's astonishment, they stopped in front of Swift's Saddle Shop.

As they opened the door, a furry ball flung itself at Ned, barking and licking and wiggling. It was Hero! After the wild greeting, Ned looked up into Morgan Swift's grinning face.

"I've been feeding him for you," said the older boy. "But I think he's awful glad to see you back again."

Ned was amazed. Morgan would do that for him? But he hardly had time to stammer his thanks before Dob Carter said, "Is your father here, Morgan? We have business to discuss."

Mr. Swift came out tying on his shop apron. "Ah, good," he said, shaking first Mr. Carter's hand, then Ned's. "I'll come right to the point, Ned. Morgan, here, is going away to attend school. I need an apprentice, someone who knows horses and harnesses. You've had experience as a driver—I think you're my man. What do you say?"

Say? Ned was speechless. He looked at his father who had a big smile on his weathered face. Dob Carter nodded.

"Yes, sir," Ned finally managed. "I'm your man."

"Good," said Mr. Swift. "You can start tomorrow."

As Ned and his father walked back down the street, with Hero panting happily alongside, Ned's thoughts were racing. He could work at the saddle shop during the day, and take care of the Orphan House horses before and after. With two jobs, maybe Pip wouldn't have to work after all.

A sense of peace flooded Ned all over. His family was back together again. Papa and Mama had both become Christians. He was learning to read. He had a job as an apprentice, learning a real trade.

Trust in God, Mr. Wesley had said.

A whole new life had just begun.

More About John Wesley

AT THE TURN OF THE EIGHTEENTH CENTURY, Samuel and Susanna Wesley were raising a large family in the parsonage of the little town of Epworth, England. On June 17, 1703, the Wesleys welcomed their fifteenth child (though not all had survived) and named him John.

John's father, Samuel, was the pastor of the village church; he was also a poet and a dreamer. Much of the burden of stretching their meager living to feed, clothe, and educate their large family was left to his wife Susanna. Two years later, baby Charles joined the already bursting parsonage—the same year that father Samuel was taken away to prison for not paying his debts.

But Susanna managed to hold things together

until her husband was released. When John was seven years old, however, the straw in the thatch roof of the parsonage caught fire (was it carelessness? or set by ruffians who had sometimes harassed the parson and his family?). Most of the family escaped quickly, but young John was trapped in the second story. Neighbors quickly came to the rescue and lifted him down from the window. Even though their home was destroyed, the Wesleys thanked God, especially for John, whom they saw as "a brand plucked from the burning." Had God saved him for some special purpose?

Susanna Wesley was a remarkable woman, with a heart for God and His work. During one of her husband's long absences in London attending to church affairs, she began holding Sunday afternoon meetings in her kitchen to tell her children, the servants, and neighbors about mission work in the East Indies. These meetings had a profound effect on John and his little brother, Charles. Susanna was also very methodical in teaching her children from the Bible. Her influence on her sons later earned her the title, "the mother of Methodism."

In 1714, at age eleven, John was sent to Charterhouse School in London to continue his education. He quickly became absorbed in the study of Latin, Greek, Hebrew, Philosophy, and Mathematics. As he reached age seventeen, he determined to go to Oxford University to continue his religious studies. A slight young man at only five feet, four inches, John Wesley didn't present an impressive figure; but he soon became known for his clear thinking, gift of writing, quick wit, and serious study.

John cut his expenses to the bone in order to stay at Oxford; but he was often tired and had a nagging cough. To improve his health he not only ate sparingly and drank only water, but he began to spend time in the open air every day, walking or swimming as the weather permitted.

Charles Wesley soon arrived at Oxford, and the two brothers gathered a group of other young men to meet together for study and discussion. By this time John had decided to become a minister, and was ordained a minister in the Church of England. He enjoyed a teaching fellowship and continued study at Lincoln College, Oxford, approaching his studies, his work, and the details of everyday life in a very disciplined, methodical manner. He was an early riser, and wrote frequently in his diaries, which he kept continuously most of his life.

At his father's suggestion, John spent two years preaching in the remote village of Wroote, near Epworth, but he felt ineffective. Returning to Oxford, he discovered that his brother Charles had formed a group of serious-minded students who wanted to worship as well as study together. The Holy Club, as it was called, was a joke to many of the other students; but it was not a joke to John, who was soon recognized as its leader. The young men visited prisoners, helping to relieve their misery, paying their small debts out of a charity fund so they could be released. The Holy Club became the core of the movement known as the Methodists.

After ten years at Oxford, John became a preacher who rode from village to village on horseback, reading a book as he rode. His life was hard, and his struggle with tuberculosis returned. Old Samuel Wesley wanted John to replace him as pastor of the little Epworth church, but even though his life would be easier, John did not feel called to use his gifts in so small a place. The same year his father died in 1735, John became excited about going to America to preach to the Indians. He arranged to travel with Colonel Oglethorpe, who had already taken two shiploads of people from debtors prisons to his colony in Georgia; Charles also went along as secretary to Oglethorpe.

When Susanna Wesley heard that her sons were traveling to a distant land as missionaries, she said, "Had I twenty sons, I should rejoice if they were all so employed."

On board ship John met a group of Moravians, a religious group from Germany, who had a calm, trusting faith that impressed the young preacher. He taught them English, while learning more about their belief in "instantaneous conversion by faith."

After four months, the little ship landed in Savannah, Georgia. Instead of going to preach to the Indians, John was appointed pastor of the colony. But his stern sermons and rigid rules won him few friends, although he experienced more success teaching the children. He lost his heart to a young woman named Miss Sophy Hopkey, but he took so long asking her to marry him that in frustration she got herself engaged to someone else, hoping to provoke him. Wounded, he backed off and didn't protest.

In the meantime, Charles had disgraced himself as Colonel Oglethorpe's secretary, and was sent back to England. John, after some bitter conflicts with various colonists, followed, feeling that his time in America was a failure.

Back in England in 1738, John struggled with the fact that his strict religious disciplines did not achieve the assurance of salvation he so longed for. On May 24, 1738, he attended a meeting in Aldersgate Street where someone read Luther's Preface to the Epistle to the Romans, describing the change which God works in the heart through faith in Christ. As he listened, John felt his heart "strangely warmed. I felt I did trust in Christ, Christ alone for my salvation; and an assurance was given me that He had taken away my sins." Charles, who had experienced a similar conversion by faith just three days earlier, gladly welcomed John's simple declaration, "I believe."

This was a turning point for the brothers, who began to travel from village to town to city all over England, Scotland, and Wales preaching and forming Methodist Societies to nurture converts. The leaders of these societies became "lay preachers," and their purpose was "To reform the nation, more particularly the Church; and to spread scriptural holiness over the land." The Wesleys never intended to begin a new church; but the doors of many Church of England churches were closed to Methodist preachers. Though John was the acknowledged leader of the Methodist movement, Charles wrote many of the hymns sung in the Methodist Societies, giving Methodism its title as "a singing religion."

George Whitefield, a friend from Oxford days, had also been turned out of the churches and began preaching in the open air. In 1739 he wrote asking John to come take his place as God called him elsewhere; the first time John preached outdoors, the crowd numbered three thousand. As he moved from place to place, he was often criticized by the official clergy who demanded to know what was his parish. John replied, "The world is my parish."

But it wasn't only the upper classes who took offense; the lower classes saw religion as a luxury for the rich and often rioted when little John Wesley rode into town. But the little giant "held steady" and gradually won the hearts of the people with his message that each person, rich or poor, had worth in God's eyes and His Son Jesus offered forgiveness and salvation to each man, woman, and child alike.

In 1742, John visited Newcastle to preach to the miners, and discovered the worst living conditions of any place he'd been in his travels. At Newcastle he established The Orphan House, which also doubled as the headquarters for the Methodist Society there. The choir at The Orphan House became one of the best in the country.

One of John Wesley's traveling companions was Grace Murray, a woman who had nursed him when he was ill, and who joined heart and soul in his ministry. John desired to marry her, but first sought the permission of his brother Charles. Rightly or wrongly, Charles (who had recently married and found himself "settling down") thought marriage would destroy his brother's effectiveness as a traveling preacher and prevented the marriage by devious means. Though John later forgave Charles, he never completely trusted his brother or relied on his judgment in the same way.

Later John rushed into marriage with a widow named Molly Vazeille, but she was jealous of his ministry and hindered him in many ways. When she left him in a huff, he did not ask her to come back, and they remained separated until her death in 1781.

John Wesley continued to travel all over England until his death at age eighty-eight on March 2, 1791. He had lived the majority of the eighteenth century, a century that witnessed the French Revolution, the American Revolution, the steam engine, machines to make cloth, and Ben Franklin's discovery of electricity. But John Wesley spent his life for God, spreading the Methodist Revival. And most of us still sing Charles Wesley's powerful hymns, such as "Hark, the Herald Angels Sing" and "O For a Thousand Tongues to Sing."